Book News

Sign up for exclusive updates and offers at
news.jljarvis.com

Get the Audiobook

jljarvis.com/highland-soldiers-the-betrayal

The Betrayal

The Betrayal

Highland Soldiers 2

J.L. Jarvis

THE BETRAYAL
Highland Soldiers 2

ISBN (ebook) 978-0-9858554-8-2
ISBN (paperback) 978-0-9858554-9-9
ISBN (audiobook) 978-1-942767-29-9

Published by BookbinderPress.com

Chapter 1

The Sword Dance

On the night before battle, a Highland chief would choose his best men for the *Ghillie Callum*, or sword dance. Each man placed two swords before him in the sign of a cross. One sword represented the soldier's own sword, and the other the sword of his enemy. As the pipes played in cadence, the dance would begin. With agile precision and power the warriors' feet would tap deftly around the crossed swords. Plaids would fly, as would the spirits of all who looked on until their hearts pounded in sync with the drum. According to legend, if a warrior's foot touched the sword, he would be wounded or killed in the battle to follow.

THE CROWD MADE room in the bailey for the dancers. The chief called out his choices, Duncan MacDonell among them. He took his place before a pair of crossed swords. Soldiers from all over Clan MacDonell land had gathered before their descent to the lowlands in service of the king. They would quell rebellious Covenanters and root out their radical leaders.

Peppered about them, small fires bathed the night in a warm amber light that caught languid ribbons of smoke. Duncan breathed in the comforting scent of charred peat while he waited for the others to get into position. One still form in the crowd drew his eye. Fair Jenny MacRuer's smile made him forget himself and smile back. By the time the reedy drone of the bagpipes slid up to their pitches, he had the good sense to look elsewhere.

The beating bodhrán drove the dancers on. Without warning, the music sped up and fueled the crowd with excitement, as cheers and cries rose with the sparks from the fire to spur on the men. Duncan MacDonell was tall and lean, with sinewy muscles that lent his masculine grace an intrinsic power. One moment he appeared nearly weightless, while the next, a force using the ground for his singular purpose. All the while, his erect bearing embodied Highland pride.

A movement from the skirts of the crowd caught his eye. A young man had drawn too close to Jenny. Duncan had seen him before. He was one of the clansmen who had just arrived. Although average in height, he was broad in the shoulders and cast an imposing presence beside Jenny. Duncan turned away as he followed the dance pattern around the swords. His heart pounded along with the drum. When he came back to face them, he remembered the name.

Tavish. The scoundrel had Jenny's hand in his grasp. She was easing her hand from his, in her too gentle way. Duncan's jaw tightened as he glared at the two of them. In that instant, he lost concentration long enough to misstep. The clang of sword against sword drew a gasp from the crowd. As the other dancers went on, Duncan stepped over the two swords and strode over to Jenny, ignoring the pats on his shoulders and back. Intercepted, he shrugged off words of support with half a nod. Soon back on course, he neared Jenny. She gave him a brief but direct look, and then turned and disappeared into the crowd. Tavish, who had been eyeing Duncan's approach, turned back to Jenny. By then, she was lost amid milling clansmen. Stopped by some friends, Duncan took a drink from a flask he was offered, and soon made an excuse to wander away.

He searched through the shadows of trees. Hurried footsteps approached from behind. Duncan's hand went to his dirk as he pivoted around.

"Duncan!" Jenny laughed and gripped his shoulders to give them a playful shake as she spoke almost tauntingly. "Were you going to fight me?"

Duncan smiled at her. His dark eyes swept down to her lips, and back up to a gaze that washed over him. "*Och*, no, darlin'. I was startled, is all."

With a sudden glance back toward the others, he took her hand and led her down the footpath to the woods. A half-moon lit their way as they walked between trees, under cover of thickening branches. He did not ask where she might wish to go, nor did she question him. They just went far enough to be cloaked in dark shadows, where he pulled her into his enveloping arms. His lips touched the strands of her wheat-colored hair as he breathed in its lavender scent.

Jenny molded her body against his and sighed. "Do you know how I'll miss you?"

Duncan opened his mouth, but any reply was lost as his rough hands met the soft skin of her neck and he tilted her chin up. Her full lips parted to meet his. Disturbed by a breeze, the pines murmured. Duncan glanced up for only an instant. With strong hands, he held her face gently and peered through the night mist at her eyes. "I've a mind to take you back into the light just to gaze at your face again."

Jenny's smile sounded in her voice. "If you dinnae ken by now what I look like—"

"I do, but I might forget while I'm away." He put his sturdy arms about her waist.

"You'd best not!" Her voice softened. "For I willnae forget you." She brushed her fingers over his cheek-bone and lips, and they kissed, hungry for all they could take before they would be forced to part.

Duncan rested his forehead against hers. "I cannae forget. You are burned in my soul." As he planted a kiss on her forehead, his hand slid down the length of her arm. Taking her hand, he led her deeper into the woods to a clearing he'd found in the daylight. A massive yew tree rested its lower branches on the ground, forming a tent to conceal them. She started to duck under the limbs, but Duncan tightened his grip, drawing her back. "Jenny." He had not meant to sound stern.

In her soft, soothing tone, Jenny said, "Have you changed your mind, Duncan?"

When he could not seem to answer, she said, "*Och*, is it that sword dance? That's a foolish superstition."

"Jenny!" He took a moment to calm himself. "Jenny, darlin', I love you."

"And I love you!" She put her arms about him and buried her face in his neck. "And I told you I want to be with you before you are gone." She took in a quick breath. "I didnae mean gone forever! You must know what I meant."

"I do." He started to smile, but the thought sobered him. But if I were to die–"

"Wheesht, I willnae hear it!" Her fingers brushed over his lips.

He grasped her hand and pressed his lips to her palm. "I want to hold you and not let you go."

Jenny reached up to smooth his troubled brow. "I'm here," she whispered. She then combed her fingers through the brown strands if his hair as her luminous eyes swept over his face.

Duncan's eyes burned into hers. "Marry me."

"You know that I will. When you get back–"

"Marry me now." He gripped her shoulders impatiently. "I'm yours. My heart, every breath, every dream for my life has you in it."

Jenny's soft blue eyes shone in the moonlight.

"Promise me." Her lips were too close not to steal a kiss. "Promise me now that you'll be mine as I have been yours for too long to remember." Her hands trembled in his. A trace of a smile formed as he lifted her hands to his lips. "Will you marry me, Jenny?"

"Yes."

"Now? Before I go?"

"Yes!" He could not see her face flush.

His eyes swept over her hair as he touched it with wonder. Moonlight filtered through leaves overhead, and obscured his vision of her. But not even night shadows could veil the soft light in her eyes.

Duncan reached into his sporran and pressed into her hand a broken coin. He matched his half to hers. "I will carry this with me. Like this coin, I'll not be whole without you." Hers had a tiny hole that was strung on a chain. "Will you wear this for me?"

As she nodded, he fastened the chain about her neck. His sure fingers lingered there for a moment. Then he untied the kertch that bound her thick hair, setting loose silken strands that spilled over her shoulders. She helped him tie the kertch around both their hands.

He peered at her. "I promise myself to you now, but in truth, I am already yours." He fought against a grin. "Whether you want me or not."

With a light laugh, Jenny said. "I am yours, and I will be forever." Her ebullience waned as she thought of his parting. "So come back to me soon, for I'll miss you." She pulled her hand from the kertch and leaned against his chest and breathed in his scent.

Duncan stroked her hair. "My Jenny. I'll be home as soon as they let me, and then we'll be together, where we belong."

She said softly, "Are we handfasted then?"

"For a year and a day."

Jenny shook off her sadness for his sake. With a glint in her eyes, Jenny winced. "*Och*, Duncan. When you say it aloud, it sounds like a very long time."

He held her at arm's length and eyed her shrewdly. "Aye, but you promised, and I'll not let you go now." He grinned and gave her a thorough hug, then he cradled her head to his chest. "When I return, we'll have a proper wedding."

Softly she said, "Not if my parents find out."

With false cheer, he hugged her close and said, "Then I shall steal you away. But you're mine, and no one—not even your parents—will keep us apart."

Jenny clutched the cloth of his leine. "Well you'll have to steal me, for I cannae make them listen to me. I'm not strong like you, Duncan."

He gazed down, and held her chin gently. "But you must be. You will be."

She lifted her eyes to meet his with a nod. He gave her that sure and easy look that always filled her with confidence.

"What's this?" Moonlight caught the tears that clung to her lashes. "Are you sorry already?"

She grinned, forcing herself to be cheerful. "I'll have plenty of time for that later."

"Oh, you will, will you?"

"Aye! But you're such a braw lad, I'd be even sorrier to lose you." Her smile faded as the thought of losing him weighed on her heart.

Duncan drew her close until their brows touched. "You'll not lose me."

She sank into the comforting crook of his neck, while he stroked her hair.

"Come, darlin'." He lifted and carried her over the threshold of the bower. The scent of the trees and the earth filled their senses as Duncan loosened his belt until it dropped with his sporran to the ground. After spreading his plaid over the bed of leaves, he unclasped Jenny's arisaid and let it fall from her shoulders. Gently, he unfastened her shift and her skirt and slid them down over her alabaster curves. Then he held his hand out to her, and she took it as he guided her down to the bed of leaves.

THE NEXT MORNING, the families and friends saw their men off. Duncan stole a glance back at Jenny, who forced a brave smile as she touched the chain round her neck that held the broken coin hiding under her shift. His last expression bore through her from a face kept void of emotion, lest anyone suspect him of stealing a glimpse of his lover. But those dark eyes sent a rush of heat to her heart. Jenny feared it would burst. Duncan's gaze drifted downward, as if he might change his mind about leaving. Abruptly, he turned and rode off with the others. When he was gone, Jenny slipped away and followed the footpath into the woods, where she found the old yew tree and sat underneath it. She touched the crushed leaves strewn over the ground. She could still feel his skin against hers.

Chapter 2

The Arrangement

JENNY AWOKE WITH A START. SHE HAD CRIED HERSELF to sleep in the woods on the bed of leaves she had shared with Duncan. The night before, she had been too full of thoughts of her future with Duncan to sleep. It was not until morning, when the men were all gone and emotions were spent, that fatigue caught up with her. She had slept here through the afternoon, and now dusk was settling. Her parents would wonder about her.

She walked home past the strips of land that her father, as tacksman, rented to farmers. Duncan's parents farmed one of these tacks, which put them beneath Jenny's station—as she had often been reminded.

Jenny stopped as her father walked out of the cottage where Duncan lived with his parents. Brodie MacDonell followed, looking unkempt and servile. He paused and put his hands on the doorframe to steady himself before following Andrew MacRuer down the footpath through the garden. Barely pausing, Brodie pleaded. Jenny did not need to hear what he said to know what it was about. In recent years, drinking had gotten the better of Brodie. Duncan kept the farm going despite his father's frequent absences. He disappeared for hours—sometimes days—only to return drunk and unfit for farm chores. They were often behind in their rent, a fact which Jenny's father never failed to point out.

"Jenny!" Her father turned back to give a gruff nod to Brodie, and turned and smiled at his daughter. Extending his arm, he said, "Come, we can walk home together."

They walked in silence until Jenny asked, "Father, is something amiss?"

With a backward glance, her father said, "They're nearly a year overdue with the rent."

Jenny hid her alarm. She wondered if Duncan knew how bad things were. "But surely Duncan will save money for rent while he's gone."

"Not enough for what they owe," said her father.

Jenny softly asked, "What are you going to do?"

"I rent the tack to make money. If they won't pay, someone else will."

"But, Father, you wouldnae put them out."

He smiled at her warmly. "Not if they pay their rent, lass. Now let's talk of pleasanter things."

Jenny opened her mouth to continue, but her father interrupted. "We're to have a visit from the MacLeans this evening."

Jenny knew who they were, and had little interest in knowing more. Mr. MacLean was a laird from a half-day's ride away. Her father looked up to the man. He had married above his own station, and was now a prosperous laird, as a result.

Jenny's father went on about Tavish, the son, but Jenny barely listened. She had always been courteous to Tavish, for it was expected. However, his growing interest in her was unsettling, so much so that she sought ways to avoid him. In the presence of wealth and power, this was easily done. Tavish valued social stature more highly than Jenny. He imposed his presence upon others, never fearing that it might be unwanted. This presumption applied doubly toward Jenny. Just last night, he had nearly dragged her away from the sword dance, never asking whether she wanted to go with him. All she had wanted was to watch Duncan and to memorize each feature, each step, and each gesture. With one last night together, no one else had mattered. It was only good fortune that had brought someone to turn Tavish's head long enough for Jenny to disappear into the crowd.

"JENNY, WHERE HAVE YOU BEEN?" Rowena MacRuer looked up from the menu she was discussing with the cook. With a nod, she handed the menu back to the cook and turned to her daughter. "*Och*, look at you! Go and fix yourself up."

Jenny lowered her chin, hiding her frown as she answered her mother. "Aye, Mum." Sometimes she wished she were not such a dutiful daughter.

Rowena gave her husband a quick peck on the

cheek and slipped her arm into his as they left the kitchen.

"Mrs. MacRuer?" A maid walked down the hallway to them.

Rowena heaved a sigh. "What is it?"

"Mrs. MacDonell is here to see you."

"To see me?"

The maid hastened to add, "Not the Lady MacDonell, but the one from the farm down the road."

Jenny was halfway to the door with a welcoming smile. She had known Duncan's mother since she and Duncan had played together as children. She was almost a second mother. After she and Duncan were married, she would be. Jenny gave Elspeth a hug, and drew back to find a face drawn with worry. Jenny's smile faded. She wanted to ask what was wrong, but she could guess what it was. Instead, she invited her into the sitting room.

"You've got things to do, Jenny," said her mother as she joined them. Jenny nodded and excused herself while her mother took over. Jenny guessed it had something to do with the rent.

Upstairs, Jenny pulled off her arisaid and leaned against the closed door. The faint scent of Duncan, fresh air and pine wafted from it. He had wrapped it around them when the night air had grown chill. Now she held it to her face and breathed in.

"JENNY!" her mother called up to her from the stairs.

The guests had arrived, and now Jenny would have to act as though she were not heartsick from missing the man she had given herself to. With a sigh, she went down the stairs to face a long evening. Her mother whispered, "They're in the sitting room. Go and make conversation." When Jenny hesitated, her mother nudged her on. A pleading stare got her nowhere, so Jenny took a fortifying breath and went in to join her father and his guests.

As she stepped into the doorway, the conversation halted. Tavish MacLean stood first, followed by his father and hers.

"Good evening," she said, looking at the three MacLeans. She looked from one to the other. "Father." She nodded and started to sit, but her mother arrived and, with a flurry of movement, ushered Jenny to Tavish's side. Jenny gave her mother a discreet, panicky glance, before turning to Tavish. "I thought you would have gone away with the others this morning."

A pointed look from her father let her know that he disapproved of her question. It was not her place to pry into decisions Tavish had made. Her job was to make him feel welcome and at ease. Jenny held her tongue, but she thought of Tavish's actions the evening before. He had not been such a gentleman when he had grabbed her and tried to force her away from the sword dance. She still felt his grip on her wrist, and resented him for it.

Tavish seemed immune to her dislike for him, as the conversation drifted along. It did so without Jenny, until she felt her mother's sharp gaze. Jenny tilted her chin up and feigned interest. As she did, her thoughts wandered once more. How had her father managed to entice the MacLeans to accept his invitation for dinner? Andrew MacRuer had long sought to renew the old friendship as a means with which he might elevate his own social standing, but his efforts had always been politely overlooked. Malcolm had been a childhood friend. When he married above his circumstances, he deliberately distanced himself from his past. However, as so many had gathered to see their men off, it made sense that they might renew their old acquaintance on this one occasion. Yet, if they had come to see Tavish off with the others, then why was he still here? As she observed him, Jenny decided she did not care enough to waste further thought on why Tavish was here. Instead, her thoughts would be better spent wishing him gone.

Tavish did know how to smile. He had all the right features to render him handsome. Unscathed by doubt or tender emotion, his face was composed of clean planes and confidence, which most women found quite appealing. Jenny was an exception, which seemed lately to draw him more fervently to her.

He turned his smile toward her. "I've delayed my departure by a day. I'll leave tomorrow to join the others."

"Oh?" Jenny nodded, eyebrows raised to approximate interest. She inadvertently met his mother's eyes, which darted along with her grin to Jenny's mother. Then the fathers joined in, glancing at each other as if they all shared an unspoken secret.

AFTER SUPPER, Jenny stood in the hallway with her parents. Her mother hissed, "Talk to her, Andrew. I cannae leave our guests all alone." With a swish of silk, she was gone.

"Father, no," Jenny whispered.

His stern face forbade opposition. "In a few minutes, Tavish MacLean is going to offer to escort you outside for a walk."

Jenny began to protest.

"Once outside, he will ask you to marry him."

"But I cannae–"

"And you will say yes." Andrew would not be moved.

"Please dinnae ask this of me," she begged quietly.

Ignoring her, he went on. "He fancies you, Jenny. You're a lucky girl."

"I am quite certain I am not the first girl he has fancied, nor will I be the last."

"But he is marrying you." Andrew smiled as he lifted her chin. "And there is no one as lovely as my wee Jenny."

She smiled but not without effort.

Andrew said, "He looked for you last night to ask you then, but he couldnae find you. Where were you?"

Jenny thought of just where she had been, in Duncan's arms, giving herself to the man that she loved. "I cannae marry Tavish."

"He delayed his departure because of you, Jenny. He was going to ask you last night."

"Last night? Did you know about this then?" Jenny

had, of course, heard of such arranged marriages, but she had never thought that her own parents would arrange a marriage without her ever suspecting it.

"Of course I knew. Now stop all this nonsense. It's all been arranged, and he's waiting for you in the sitting room."

"I cannae marry him," she said meekly.

"Oh, but you can, and you will."

"No." Jenny felt physically ill. She had never been able stand up to her father. What he saw as respect was, in truth, simple fear. It was easier to obey than to lose his approval. But now she had to risk it. What choice was there?

She had wanted to sound firm, but her words came out breathless and hushed. "I am promised to someone, to Duncan. We are handfasted."

Andrew's face grew red as he spoke with quiet restraint. "You promised yourself? To him?"

"I did." Jenny felt the same fear she used to feel as a child, when she had done something wrong.

He stared at her. "Duncan? That drunkard's son?"

"Father, please don't be cruel."

"Pardon me. Farmer. One who is too busy tipping the bottle to farm his land so he can pay his rent. Is that the life you want?"

"Duncan isnae like that."

"He sent his wife over to beg your mother for more time to pay rent."

"His father did that, not Duncan."

Andrew shook his head. "I'll not have that for my wee Jenny."

"I'm not your wee Jenny anymore." She spoke too

quickly, and revealed too much. Too late, she reined in her emotions.

Jenny's mother slipped back through the sitting room door as Andrew said, "When was this handfast?"

"Last night."

Andrew drew close and gripped her jaw. After a long silence, he forced her chin up. With dread, Jenny lifted her eyes.

"Did he bed you?"

"Andrew!" said her mother, signaling for him to hush.

"Look at me and tell me the truth."

In her father's eyes, she saw not only anger but fear mixed with disgust, which grew stronger with each moment she failed to answer him.

"No," Jenny lied.

The deep sigh of relief that came from him nearly frightened her more than his anger. He let go of her chin.

"And who witnessed this handfasting?"

"No one. But it's still just as true."

Andrew leveled a gaze of cold steel. "If no one saw it, it cannae be proven."

"No one needs to prove it! He knows, and I know. Nothing will change that!"

Andrew's quiet words belied his seething anger. "He'll most likely be gone for more than a year and a day, so your handfast means nothing."

"It means everything to me."

Andrew went on as though he had not heard her. "Right now, you are going to walk into that room and smile sweetly. And when he invites you for a walk, you will smile again and go with him. And when he asks you to marry him, you'll say yes. For if you do not, I will throw Duncan's parents out of their miserable hovel."

"Father, you cannae!"

"How do you think they will manage? I'll tell you. They won't."

Jenny asked, "How could you do such a thing?"

"I will do anything to protect my daughter."

"I dinnae want protecting from Duncan. I love him."

"Then think, Jenny, for you will bear the weight of the consequences."

"You ask too much of me."

"I ask you to do what is best."

Andrew was calm. He had won.

Jenny knew he would do it, and she knew it would kill Duncan's mother to lose her home. The poor woman had suffered for years with a husband who did little to keep the farm going. Now, with Duncan away, her life would be even harder. The land would be hers to farm nearly alone.

"Duncan willnae stand for this," Jenny protested.

"Duncan willnae know."

"*Och*, do you not think I'll tell him the moment he's back?"

"Yes, I do." Andrew paused, a smug smile forming. "But, you see, I am letting them stay there. It's a generous offer, one which I will withdraw if Duncan ever finds out what I've told you. So, my dear one, you are free to tell him, just as I am free to throw the whole lot of them out of their home."

Jenny was stunned. She knew her father was ruthless in business matters, but she never expected him to treat her like this. If Duncan were here, he would know what to do. He would stand up to her father, take care of his parents, and marry her. But Duncan was gone, and the fate of his parents now lay on her shoulders. If she refused to marry Tavish, Duncan's parents would lose their home. Without Duncan, they would be helpless. His father would drink, and his mother would suffer. After years of hard work, she was in no condition to travel on foot searching for work and a home.

If Jenny went against her father, he might throw her out, too. Where would she go? She could try to find Duncan, but how? He was in the lowlands, but where? Even if she knew more, she had no idea how she would get there. No proper lady would travel alone, nor would she know how. All of her life had been focused on becoming accomplished. She had learned how to sing and do needlework, neither of which would see her safely through the rough Highland terrain. In her quest to find Duncan, she could lose him forever.

Jenny faced a hard truth. Without a home, Duncan's parents might not survive the winter. At all cost, she had to keep Duncan's parents safe until his return. As for Jenny, there would be no wedding yet. Tavish was leaving to catch up with the rest of the men. He would return with the others, Duncan included. After that, she and Duncan would find a way out.

With Jenny now quiet, Andrew smiled and kissed

her on the forehead. "That's my Jenny." He led Jenny back into the sitting room.

Tavish led Jenny outside for a walk. As they went down the garden path, his hand drifted toward hers. To evade it, she reached up to brush her hair from her face. They followed the path around and a birch tree, where Tavish stopped and lifted her hand. She could not make herself look at him.

"Jenny." Tavish studied her, seeking her full attention. "They must have told you that we are to be married."

"Only just." She glanced at him long enough to be polite. She could not hold his gaze. Her thoughts centered upon Duncan and his family. She reminded herself that she had to buy time until Duncan returned.

"I'll be leaving tomorrow to join the other men."

In that moment, the thought struck her. Duncan was one of those men. Tavish would join them and tell them. Then Duncan would know. He would learn of the wedding, but never know why. She had no way to tell him. Even if she could get a message to him, she could not tell him now—not without putting his parents at risk. She was going to break his heart, just as hers was broken already.

Tavish said, "When I return, we'll be married. Jenny, do you hear what I'm saying?"

"Aye," her voice broke.

Misreading it as a sign she was moved, Tavish smiled.

Jenny fixed her eyes downward, hoping he would say what he had to say quickly.

"We'll be married, and you'll be my wife."

She inwardly cringed.

He stepped closer and kissed her. She had not expected a kiss, although she supposed that she should have. Nor had she expected his tongue to seek a way past her closed lips. As she drew back, Tavish slipped his palm behind her head and resisted. By reflex, she gasped.

"You're to wed me. Now gie us a kiss." His eyes burned as claimed her lips with a devouring kiss. There was no escaping his mouth or his serpentine tongue.

"Tavish." She pressed her palms to his chest and pulled away.

He released her but appeared bewildered, yet not too much to stare at her mouth. "You're so very bonnie. You hardly can blame a lad for wanting to kiss his sweetheart before he goes off to war."

She discreetly wiped his kiss from her lips with her fingers. "It isnae quite war that you're going to, Tavish."

His eyes narrowed. "Take a care, my love, lest you sound like a harpy."

Now indignant, Jenny looked up, her lips parted in protest.

To her surprise, Tavish's mouth spread to a grin. "You've a bit of fire in you, girl. I like that." His hungry eyes bore through her as he leaned down to kiss her.

Jenny started to turn, but he took her jaw in his hands.

"Tavish…" She tried to hold him at bay, but he was strong and insistent. "I pray you, grant me some time."

He released her with scorn. "Time for what, Jenny?"

"I barely know you." She wanted to weep or vomit but managed to do neither. "I've only just found out we're to be married."

"You'll have your time after I'm gone. Until then, I'll have a proper kiss." And he took it.

THE NEXT MORNING, Tavish rode off with the handful of men who had stayed behind with him. Jenny donned a brave face and wondered. How long would it be before Duncan found out? A few days? A week? What did it matter? He would find out. When he did, he would be certain that she had betrayed him.

Chapter 3

The Homecoming

Jenny had had more than a year to prepare for this day. Yet there were times when it seemed like her betrothal to Tavish was just a bad dream. While Duncan and Tavish were away fighting for the king against Covenanters, the days had slipped by with no change. No one knew when the men would return, if at all. The pain of such thinking drove her to set plans for the future aside. She had never intended to go through with the wedding, and yet she had spent more than a year making plans with her parents. All the while, she yearned for Duncan. She had broken his heart, and hers with it. But their love was still true. They would find their way back together. After that, Duncan would know what to do. Until then, the wedding plans remained in place. As the months passed, it seemed less and less real, until Jenny found it easy to set thoughts of marriage aside.

Then the men came home. Word spread quickly as

everyone gathered to welcome them. Most of the soldiers would stop here for a meal, a dram, and some rest, before continuing on to their homes, so a growing crowd of nearby families was ready to greet their loved ones. In its midst, Jenny stood, and she watched their arrival with anxious eyes.

From beside her, came a voice. "Hello, Jenny."

She had not wished to remember the voice, but she did. "Tavish." She turned, sure she had managed to hide her disappointment, but a fleeting light in his eyes proved her wrong. "I didnae see you," she said, forcing a smile. How would she have noticed him? She had been watching for Duncan.

They talked of the journey, the weather—anything but what was really on their minds. Her parents joined them and took over the conversation, which eased Jenny's discomfort. Tavish would stay at their house for the night, before riding on to his home.

Jenny spied Duncan's friend, Alex, and excused herself to go to him. He stood out from a crowd, not for his beauty. He was almost too rugged to be handsome. But his quiet presence compelled those about him to take notice, for he had a strength that was as much mind as muscle.

"Alex!" Jenny put her hand on his arm. When he turned to face her, she saw something was wrong.

"Jenny."

She continued to smile, but her eyes betrayed her. "Is Duncan with you?"

"No."

Dread drained the color from her face. Her lips formed the beginning of a question. "Steady, lass." His chilled manner now gone, Alex grasped her upper arm to support her.

"Are you alright, Jenny?" A concerned Tavish had joined them.

Jenny said, "Yes, I'm fine. Just a bit overwhelmed."

Tavish studied her.

As Alex released her arm, she said, "Did everyone— is everyone with you?"

"Come, Jenny," said Tavish. He turned and took her hand to lead her away as though she were a child.

Jenny turned back to Alex and whispered, "Where is Duncan?"

He and Duncan were part of a close group of friends who had grown up together, with Jenny like a sister among them. The men went on to train and fight together.

Alex took note, not only of Jenny's hushed agitation, but also of Tavish's watchful insistence. Alex proceeded to fill Jenny in on the news of their friends. Callum stood nearby with a raven-haired beauty beside him. He was the chief's son, although for years unacknowledged. He had brought home a wife from the lowlands. Tongues had wagged for weeks over that, but Hughie's mother, Nellie, assured everyone that Mari was lovely, both inside and out, and that Callum was lucky to have found her. Behind Callum, their friend Charlie turned to embrace one of the many young women who seemed to fall under his charm almost daily. It was hard to fault him for his confidence, when his mere smile made women blush. His coarse sand-colored hair and square jaw made them stare, while his powerful build and bearing made knees weak.

Impatient, Tavish said, "My parents are waiting." He tugged her along for a few steps, as Jenny looked back. They had spoken of everyone except Duncan. Tavish stopped. Jenny nearly bumped into him. The next moment, he was talking with someone else. Now distracted, he released Jenny's hand.

Jenny took a discreet step toward Alex. "What has happened to Duncan?"

"Calm yourself, lass." He eyed Tavish warily.

With Tavish beside her, Jenny could not explain herself. Alex would not know of her love for Duncan. She and Duncan had hidden their feelings from their friends, for fear the inevitable teasing might ruin what they shared. But as their love deepened and they knew they would marry someday. Jenny had confided in her mother. That had been a mistake. When her father heard of it, he made it clear that nothing would come of it. It was a childhood fancy that would pass. From then on, she and Duncan kept their love secret from everyone.

Alex cast a level gaze at her frantic eyes and quietly said, "Nothing has happened. He is well." His eyes flickered toward Tavish, still talking.

Jenny exhaled and clung to what was left of her composure.

Alex said, "He took a job on a merchant ship."

"He didnae come home with you?"

"No."

"How long will he be gone?"

Alex leveled a frank look. "I dinnae think that he's very eager to come home just yet."

Before Jenny could respond, Alex's sister flew into his arms. His brothers and parents surrounded him, while Tavish led her away toward his parents.

THE NEXT MORNING, Tavish was gone, but he promised to return in a week to see Jenny. He did, and he returned every week for a month. Talk of the wedding was relentless. When would Duncan come home? The wedding was one month away.

She escaped to the woods and the shelter of the yew tree where she and Duncan had spent their last evening together. Over the past year, she had often come here to feel closer to Duncan. Here she could think of him, free of the lie of her betrothal to Tavish. For a year, she had thought about how it would end. Jenny leaned back and gazed up at the sheltering branches, and then shut her eyes to daydream. She had to believe that Duncan would return to her. With one look, he would know that her love had not changed. She would tell him the truth, and he would understand. Before her father could evict his parents, they would all run away, and life would be as they always had hoped.

Jenny walked out of the woods. A mist hovered over the ground, with scattered clear patches drifting on the crisp autumn breeze.

"Jenny?" He came out of the haze.

"Tavish."

"One of the farmers' lads thought they saw you heading this way." He grinned. "I've decided to stay one more day."

In her dismay, Jenny failed to watch where she was going and stumbled on a tree root. Tavish took hold of her arm to steady her, and left his hand there as they walked through the mist.

The path led past Duncan's cottage. She did not expect to see him come around the corner of the byre and stop. Why had no one told her he was home? His deep-set eyes locked on hers. Jenny opened her mouth as if to speak, even though they were too far away to do so. Duncan's eyes darted to Tavish and his arm on Jenny's arm. His dark, troubled eyes held her transfixed. Duncan turned from her abruptly and went into the byre. He was gone, and still she could not take her eyes from the spot where she had first seen him.

"Jenny?" Tavish stared.

Distracted, she looked up at him.

"Stop staring. You disgrace yourself and make me look a fool." With a tug, he led her on down the path.

She forced her attention toward home, but her heart and her thoughts were with Duncan.

Chapter 4

The Storm

DUNCAN SURVEYED THE FIELD HE HAD LEFT TO HIS father's care. The tacksman, Jenny's father, had already come calling to ask for the overdue rent. Duncan's father was gone, as he was most days, leaving Duncan and his mother to run the farm and answer for the unpaid rent. His mother would not cry in front of Duncan, so he left her that morning with a cup of tea and a kiss on the forehead, and then went outside to work out his anger. The untended field contained little that was fit to harvest, other than a patch of vegetables his mother had planted and tended, so he went to the byre to put things in order. It appeared as though no one had touched it since he had left for the lowlands. Anyone else might have cursed, but Duncan had expected little more of his father. He clenched his teeth and put his mind and his muscles to cleaning the mess. In the midst of mucking out the stables, he heard Jenny say his name softly from inside the doorway.

Duncan was not one to reveal his feelings. Perhaps

he had learned by example. His father hid feelings inside a bottle, while his mother concealed hers with stoic perseverance. One would think nothing fazed her, but that would be wrong. She had passed on her pride and her dogged restraint to her son. Duncan hid what he felt were weak shows of emotion with steely control, which was now being tested. Just the sound of Jenny's voice pierced the thin shield he had hewn to prepare for this moment. It was not pride that kept him from turning to face her. It was his heart, which he could not rein in. He would not let her see him like this. Yet, as much as she had hurt him, his heart would not give up. It would seek out the pain that would crush it. And so, with tenuous control, he convinced himself that it was better to face her now, in this place, than in public. He filled one more shovel and heaved it to the barrow, before turning to face her.

Turning was one thing. Even meeting her eyes was within the bounds of courtesy, but to fix his eyes on hers was wholly unwise. There was no helping it. Love pulled him to her and overpowered months of bitterness that should have protected him by now.

"Jenny." His polite manner put distance between them. He saw that it stung, and he took some pleasure in it.

"How are you?" Jenny asked meekly.

With that, his pain soured. Duncan let out a bitter laugh, which threw Jenny off guard. With forced cheer, he leaned on his shovel, eyes gleaming with rancor. "I'm fine, Jenny. Thank you for asking. And you?"

She was visibly hurt.

"How are you, Jenny? And how are the wedding

plans coming?" Without waiting for her answer he turned away and propped the shovel against the wall. There he took a moment to stare at the stone wall and seethe.

When the silence grew too much for her, Jenny said his name softly.

"Why have you come here?" He turned to face her.

"I'm sorry that you had to find out from somebody else."

"Tavish."

"Sorry?"

"I found out from Tavish."

"*Och*, Duncan. I'm sorry. He didnae know about us."

"Of course he didnae know. No one did. That's what made it so easy for you."

"Nothing's been easy for me."

A dark look clouded his eyes, but he tamped down his feelings and shrugged. "You've made a good match. A laird's son. You've come up in the world." Duncan cast a disparaging glance about his own byre. "Although, I'll admit I was surprised when they told me. I never knew that was what you wanted. I thought—" Duncan stopped and seemed almost to smile to himself. "Well, it doesn't matter what I thought." His face drained of expression, until all that remained was a stony stare. "Good luck to you, Jenny."

"Duncan, I—"

Before she could go on, Duncan turned away and resumed working. "Goodbye, Jenny," he said, as he scooped with his shovel and filled up the barrow.

ALEX AND DUNCAN went down to Loch Oich to fish for some salmon for supper. Duncan cursed as one got away.

Alex kept his gaze on the lake. "You're in a right foul mood."

"Aye."

They stood quietly fishing. Alex glanced over at Duncan. "I have not seen you like this since Edinburgh. It isnae Mari still, is it?"

"Mari? No." Duncan stared at the water. "It never really was Mari."

Alex watched the water and waited.

"At the time, I was trying to forget. But there they were. Callum and Mari were so much in love, and I'd lost what they had. At times it was torment to see it."

The thought settled in silence between them for a moment, and then Alex asked, "Have you seen Jenny yet?"

"Jenny." He knew it was coming, but the sound of her name made his heart ache.

Alex's expression was too knowing to ignore, and yet Duncan tried. "I have." Even as he said it, his composure crumbled.

Alex would not be deterred. "We all knew there was something between you and Jenny."

Duncan took in a breath to protest, but exhaled with a rueful nod.

Alex asked, "How could we not?"

"We were friends, she and I."

"Friends?" Alex looked doubtful.

Duncan gazed at the lake. "Aye, that's how it began."

"Friends who fell in love," Alex said, completing the thought.

"Well, I did, anyway. All she did was promise to marry me."

Alex cast a sharp look of concern. "We never knew that. We would see you steal glances at each other, but... marriage..." Alex slowly shook his head.

"We were handfasted. On the night before we all left, we promised to love one another forever, and I meant it. We were going to have a kirk wedding when I came home. And the next week, along comes Tavish MacLean strutting about camp and boasting to all who would listen–including me, to my misfortune–that they were betrothed." Duncan swallowed his pain. "She gave her body to me, except for her hand. That she gave to Tavish MacLean."

Alex said, "I dinnae understand. Why would she do it?"

"Well, I am braw and handsome." Duncan let out a laugh that soon faded. "But I am not the son of a laird." Duncan thought of whose son he was.

"She cannae love him," said Alex.

"What does it matter? I cannae have her." He looked at Alex. "It's taken me over a year to come up with that brilliant conclusion."

With a sympathetic smile, Alex said, "Aye, well you are a powerful thinker."

Duncan laughed, in spite of himself. "Not long after that, I met Callum's Mari. I saw what they had. It was what I had lost. And I was lonely for it. I saw Mari with Callum, and I fell in love with the way that she loved him. She was devoted to him, and still is."

"Unlike Jenny," Alex said quietly.

"Just so." Duncan gazed at the lake and exhaled. "We will starve at this rate."

"It's too early for salmon," said Alex.

With a wry look, Duncan said, "I believe I said just that on our way down here."

"But did you not miss the fishing here while we were gone?" Alex grinned.

"This isnae fishing. It's standing in water."

Alex laughed. "Well, perhaps we could pack up and go have a dram."

Without hesitation, Duncan turned and waded back to the shore, calling behind him, "You have renewed my faith in your wisdom."

JENNY WALKED with her mother to the village to shop in the mercat square. Her father had already left very early to look at some cattle and hogs. Vendors were selling their wares from pushcarts. People bartered and chattered, and all was a clamor of color and move-ment. Once one of her favorite pastimes, she now found herself walking with no more purpose than to listen and respond to her mother when needed.

From moment to moment, she hoped to see Duncan. He would not want to see her, but if she could just gaze at him unnoticed, her heart might not ache so. She longed for a glimpse of the masculine grace of his walk, his dark hair and deep eyes that always seemed remote unless they regarded her. She used to watch him when he was not aware, and she would wonder if anyone would ever get close to his heart. He had always been standoffish, but not out of arrogance. Behind his aloof manner he was caring and kind. Few people knew him well, but those who did found little fault. Acquaintances respected his character. Foes in battle faced his fearsome skill with a sword, but Jenny knew his heart and his passion. She knew also what he must think of her. Part of her hoped, in some way, he might hold onto his faith in her and discern her dilemma. But how could he? Short of reading her mind, there was nothing left for him to think, but that she had cast him aside in favor of Tavish. Tavish had social standing, which Duncan did not. Still, she wanted to believe that he knew her better than to think this would sway her. Her heart sank. How it must have hurt Duncan to come home to the burden of his family's debt. That weight, alone, was enough. But to lose Jenny to Tavish must have hurt deeply. For that, Jenny had no cure. She had already come too close to telling the truth. She had never stopped loving him, nor would she. She had done what was best for his parents. She had to be strong and not tell him until she found a way to convince her father to call off the wedding.

JENNY'S MOTHER chatted with a baker while he wrapped up some tarts.

While they talked, Jenny planned her escape. One

of them would have to take a breath soon. "Mum, my head is aching. Would you mind if I walked home?"

"There were a few more things I was hoping to get, but I suppose they could wait." Her mother's eyebrows creased as she stared off to the distance and thought.

"You stay," Jenny insisted. "I'll walk home. 'Tis not far, and I think a walk may help."

Rowena smiled gently and touched her daughter's forehead and cheek. "Alright. But lie down when you get home. I willnae be long here."

Jenny passed by Duncan's mother and her friend Nellie, who were waiting for a draper to measure out four ells of cloth. Jenny greeted them warmly and continued toward home. Duncan joined them, leading his horse as he walked through the mercat.

Nellie gave him a hug. "I've not spent more than a few minutes with you since I left for home from the fighting. You must come by for a visit. I've missed you, lad."

Duncan smiled. "I've missed you, too, Nellie." He turned to his mother. "While we were in the lowlands, Nellie made us feel as though we were home."

Nellie's eyes misted up. "I wish I had stayed a bit longer." With a sigh, she said, "Ah, well. If wishes were horses, poor men would ride." Nellie squeezed Duncan's arm. "Look at me—and on such a fine day." She glanced up with false cheer. "*Och*, I spoke too soon. Do you see those clouds? I'd best be on my way home."

Duncan's mother asked him to pack a few of her heavier items on his horse. "Nellie, can we carry something for you?"

"I've already given Charlie the bulk of it. But you could do one thing for me, Elspeth."

"Aye?"

Nellie nodded. "Stop for a cup of tea on your way home."

"There is nothing I would enjoy more." Elspeth smiled warmly.

Lightening flashed, followed in an instant by thunder and the crack of a tree as it fell.

Both flinched. Nellie said, "Did we not see Jenny walking that way?"

Duncan looked toward the tree, where Jenny must be.

Elspeth studied him for a moment. In a quiet voice, she said, "Duncan, we're closer to her than anyone else, and you've got your horse."

He started to shake his head, but she urged him. "Go to her."

RELIEVED TO BE ALONE with her thoughts, Jenny reached the outskirts of the village. Her heart was with Duncan, and hiding that fact was a burden. A mile from her house, thick clouds rolled in to darken the sky. She quickened her pace as a few drops of rain fell. Wild gusts whipped her arisaid about as she held it close to her chin. Lighting flashed. Thunder bellowed. With a deafening crack, a tree split down the middle and started to fall. Jenny ran, but her foot caught a deep rut in the road and she fell. The tree barely missed her as it landed across the road. By now, rain was pelting her, drowning the sound of the hoof beats. She struggled to stand as her ankle buckled beneath her. Rivulets of water streamed about her feet as she gripped limbs of the fallen tree for support.

"Jenny!"

She glanced up to see Duncan on horseback. "Are you hurt?"

"*Och*, it's my ankle. I twisted it when I fell."

"I'll take you home."

"Dinnae worry about me."

Ignoring her protest, he leapt down and lifted her onto his horse, then mounted behind her.

The storm was as violent as it was sudden. Jenny gripped the edge of the saddle, but there was no need. Duncan circled her waist and held her securely against him as they rode through pelting rain for the last mile to her house.

Held against his strong shoulders and chest, she felt safe and sure. She had missed his warmth and his touch. She could almost forget what had torn them apart—enough so, that she let herself imagine how it might be to flee with him now. What if they ran away? She could tell him the truth. There was nothing to stop them. But that was not true. If they ran away, her father would evict Duncan's parents. With no home and no place to go, his parents' lives would be ruined. If she were lucky, she might find work in Glasgow or Edinburgh, never seeing daylight as she worked from dawn until well after dark. Duncan's father would try, but he would be as he always had been, a dreamer who would never find his way past a drink or the next chance to gamble. Duncan's mother would never complain, but the burden would fall on her, and the weight would wear her down, if not crush her. That would be the price for Jenny's happiness, and it was too great. She could never tell Duncan. He would not let her go. He would insist upon shouldering the burden for them all, but he was in no position to do so. Her father would turn them all out. With no home and no means of support, even if she and Duncan could manage, it would be too hard on his parents. In time, Duncan would grow to resent her, for she would have been the cause of their hardship. Without her, their lives would go on undisturbed. Every time she tried to find a way out of the trap she was in, she wound up back here in its snare, her heart breaking. The best thing for Duncan and his family would be to go on with their lives without her.

So Jenny tried to sear into her memory what she could never have: Duncan's arms about her as they were at this moment, the palm of his hand on her waist, and how close his mouth was to hers. If she turned, her lips would meet his. In another time, she might have kissed him on a whim, unconcerned about whether such a moment would come again. But now, she had lost her true love, but her heart would not break. Poets would have people believe that hearts broke, but they did not. They beat on, and with each beat, they ached without mercy.

They reached the stable. Duncan helped Jenny down from his horse. Her breath caught as his hands gripped her waist and she slid down against him. But her feet touched the ground, and the strong hands were gone.

Duncan turned and ran to swing open the doors, and they rushed inside. "That was a terrible storm to go walking in," he told her, as he checked his horse's hooves for stones.

With longing, Jenny took in the sight of his broad shoulders and muscular arms. "I didnae see it coming. It was good luck that brought you to me."

Duncan busied himself tending to his horse. Without looking up, he said, "It wasnae luck. My mother saw you leaving the village as the storm clouds blew in. When we heard the tree fall, she and Nellie sent me after you."

"Oh." Although she had no right to be, Jenny was disappointed that it had not been his idea. "Well, thank them for me."

At last, he leveled a gaze, and her heart missed a beat. They had known one another too long and too well not to see more in a glance than either might wish to reveal. Duncan could not have missed her reaction, but he turned away and spoke as if to a stranger. "I'd have done it for anyone."

"I know," she said, watching him still. She could not help herself. His wet leine clung to his muscles as if to taunt her with how it would feel to touch him and know every part of that body again.

With a nod toward the door, Duncan said, "Can you walk on that ankle?" His gaze lingered until he caught himself and looked outside at the rain.

"It hurts a wee bit, but I can walk." Jenny wished she had lied, but it was not in her nature. He would have known if she had.

"Go inside. I'll leave as soon as the storm lets up."

"Would you like some hot tea?" Jenny asked. Her voice had its old lilt, but the light in her eyes was lost behind a soft veil of sorrow that fluttered away when his eyes would not meet hers.

Duncan glanced toward the house and shook his head. "I'm sure I was seen coming here. It would not do for me to be found in there alone with–"

Her candid gaze met his. They were lost in that gaze for a moment.

Duncan finished his thought. "–with a woman about to be married."

They both looked at the house. What might have been on a day such as this, before they had learned that their love had no more substance than mist?

Jenny said, "I've wanted to explain to you."

"No, dinnae talk of it now." His eyes darted toward the house for only a moment with a hard expression.

"But Duncan–"

"No, Jenny," he snapped.

Jenny flinched. Seeing this, Duncan lowered his voice. "Go inside." He stared at the house.

She hesitated. "I don't like to leave you out here."

"But you're so good at it." He smiled with cold eyes. "I've grown used to being alone." He had not meant to sound angry, but the words had slipped out.

Jenny looked down as she measured her words. "Duncan, I wish..." but the only words that would come, could not be spoken.

"Aye, so do I."

The rain had nearly stopped. Gentle drops clung and some fell from the eaves. He gave her one last fleeting glance that landed like a blunt blow. Turning, he tightened his horse's girth and led it outside. Jenny watched, taking in every muscle that flexed in his shoulders and back, and his large hands that were gentle and sure. She nearly called out his name. But what was there to say?

Unwilling to wait for the rain any longer, Duncan mounted his horse. He looked down at her with eyes that were not harsh, as she had expected, but hollow. She yearned to reach out to hold him and tell him the truth. She could not, so she looked down to hide it. "You have every reason to hate me."

With forced calm, he said, "Goodbye, Jenny."

As he rode down the road, Duncan said softly, "I wish that I could hate you, darlin'."

Chapter 5

The Patron Saint of the Sea and Sailors

Saint Michael was the patron saint of the sea and the sailors. No one had spent more time at sea than Duncan, so when Michaelmas came at the end of September, Alex made it his mission to lift Duncan's spirits by including him in every toast. Had it not been Michaelmas, Alex would have found some other excuse, for he had watched Duncan brood long enough. With the help of friends Callum and Charlie, Alex made sure that Duncan gave due honor to St. Michael.

With a resounding thud, Duncan set down his cup. "Lads, I'll have some of that cake over there."

When Duncan's balance failed him for a moment, Alex eyed him, amused. "Are you sure you can walk?"

"And why can't I?"

Alex grinned. "No reason, really. But just for the sake of conversation, lad, how many drams have you had?"

Duncan shrugged. "Two or three."

The lads did not even try to hide their amusement.

Duncan tripped. "Maybe four." He waved off Charlie's offer of help, an offer that came with a laugh. Duncan recovered and stepped carefully onward, with Charlie and Alex behind at the ready to prop him upright. In truth, they were only a bit more sure-footed than he.

They lingered beside a table of cakes, where Charlie steadied Duncan. Callum leaned over to Alex. "Do you think you might have overdone it a wee bit?"

Alex shrugged. "Overdone what? Helping him to forget?"

"Forget what? How to walk? Aye, you've done that."

"The trouble with you, Callum, is that your sweet wife has tamed you." Alex shook his head with mock regret. "I can barely recall the man you once were."

"*Och*, let me help you then." Callum reached out to box Alex's ears.

Alex dodged out of his way with a laugh. "See? You've gone soft! The old Callum wouldnae have missed."

"I was just showing you pity." Callum smirked as he turned away.

Alex laughed even harder. "Mari, come here and behold what's become of this man of yours."

Mari smiled. "Oh, I ken what's become of him, and I like it just fine. He's a braw man, and I love him."

Callum scooped Mari into his arms and spun her about before burying his face in her neck. As he growled and planted a kiss there, Mari attempted to loose herself from his sturdy arms. "Callum, people are looking!" And yet, as she said it, she failed to hide a slight smile.

"Good God, Callum, you beast." Alex said, feigning disgust. "Mari, will you not come to your senses and leave this oaf?"

Callum released her enough to circle his arm about her waist and gaze fondly at her.

She met his eyes with an equal measure of warmth. "My senses are just fine where they are." Mari played with the open neckline of Callum's leine, their gazes locked.

Alex cleared his throat. "You two know I'm still here, do ye not?"

They laughed and turned toward him as Charlie appeared with Duncan lagging behind. Charlie grabbed Alex's shoulder to pull him away toward some new attraction. Knowing Charlie, Alex had no doubt that it involved women. They passed some horses and riders about to race. Alex started to watch, but Charlie pulled him along. "We've more important things to do. We're going to find Duncan a woman." Charlie clapped his hand on Duncan's shoulder. "What color hair would you like?"

They drew close to the music and dancing and stopped. Duncan said, "Light."

"Light isnae a color," Charlie said as he flashed a dimpled grin at a pretty girl standing with two of her friends.

Duncan caught sight of Jenny as Tavish swept her into a new dance. "Light like the barley before harvest, when the wind whispers through it in waves."

"Well that's specific," said Alex, with a knowing expression. In the soft glow of sunset, the dancers moved about in their pattern. There Jenny was, dancing and smiling, and Tavish danced with her.

Charlie's glance swept from Alex to Duncan. His face brightened. In an instant, he was gone, but returned minutes later with two grinning girls. "I'm afraid, Alex, you'll have to fend for yourself."

Alex leveled a look and said, "I'm quite sure I can manage without you."

Charlie laughed as he nudged Duncan toward one girl and swept the other into his arms for a lively High-land Schottische. Duncan's partner seemed eager enough to hold him close to secure his unsteady balance on the turns. In spite of the whisky, Duncan's body responded by instinct and memory to the steps and turns of the dance and the touch of a woman. The music stopped. Just as suddenly, Duncan told his partner that he had to go.

"Where? I'll come with you." She took hold of his hand and caught up to his pace.

With eyes fixed forward, Duncan said, "I have to go." He stopped and gently pried her hand from his.

"Oh! Well, I'll wait for you here."

He opened his mouth to protest, but he had more pressing business. With a shrug, he walked off toward some shrubbery to relieve himself.

When he returned, she was in the same spot with the same eager smile. He smiled and wandered away, but his new companion caught up and slipped her arm into his as she pressed her plump curves against him.

Lifting round eyes to his, she said, "I've something

to show you." Sliding her hands down his arms, she clasped his hand.

In a few steps, they were within the dark cover of trees and thick bracken. Wasting no time, she slipped her hands over the edge of his belt and gently pulled him against her and guided his hands about her waist.

Reaching up on her tiptoes, she started to kiss him, but he gripped her waist and held her at bay. "No, lass. You dinnae want me."

"*Och*, but I do."

Duncan shook his head and watched leafy shadows move over her features. "I've got nothing for you."

"That isnae true, Duncan." With a coy downward glance down past his belt, she said, "You've got something I'd like very much. And I like you. I always have." Her eyes rose to meet his, full of feelings he could not return. If she gave him her body, she would want his heart in return. She deserved as much, but he could not give it.

He paused to find words that would not have too sharp a sting. If they were there, the whisky obscured them. "I'm sorry."

"What is it? Am I not bonnie enough?" She glanced away, but Duncan touched her chin and lifted it gently. "You are very bonnie, and I am a fool. But I've been wounded, and there's no help for it."

"Wounded?" Her eyes went straight to his groin. "There was nothing wounded there moments ago. What you need is someone who appreciates you." She began to appreciate him with her hands, and his body responded even as he backed away from her.

She reached out, but he held her gently at arm's length. "We must go back now."

"No, Duncan."

Her round sad eyes cajoled him, but a warm smile was all he would offer. "Come, bonnie lass, will you dance with me?"

She reluctantly took the hand that he offered, and followed him back toward the others.

"Duncan?"

"Aye, lass?"

"You've nae said my name once."

His eyes shut for an instant before he dared meet the frown that awaited him.

She pushed his arm away. "You dinnae remember me, do you?"

He thought hard, but it would not come to mind. "Of course I do."

"Good, then tell me my name."

"I'm sorry. 'Tis the whisky."

"The whisky?" Her look condemned him.

Cold silence hovered between them until they arrived at the edge of a small crowd that circled the dancing.

She said, "Rose." When he tried to act as though it were familiar, she shook her head. "It's been Rose since we were wee *bairns*."

He glanced toward the people dancing and laughing, but she drew his attention back. "You once found me picking berries, and you walked home with me. A wild rose bloomed from the hedgerow, and you plucked it and gave it to me. I know you were having fun, but I kept it." She glanced back at his blank face.

He did not remember. "Men like you laugh and say nice things. You're the most dangerous kind, for you dinnae know what you do to a girl."

Duncan was baffled. Charlie, yes, but he was not like that. He would not have played with hers or anyone else's affections as she was accusing. It was not in his nature. He cupped her face in his hands and said, "You're right, Rose. You deserve better than me." He kissed her forehead. It was meant to be kind, but she gave him a petulant look and then walked away.

As he tried to make sense of what had just happened, Duncan turned and caught Jenny's eye. Their gazes locked for a moment as Tavish led her into the center to dance. Duncan watched, unable to do anything else. As if sensing his thoughts and his lingering gaze, Jenny turned toward him with a pleading expression that both tugged at his heart and confused him. He turned away so she would not catch him watching again. It was then that he saw Rose heading straight toward him. He glanced back at Jenny and ducked into the shadows before Rose could catch up.

Soon after, Duncan's mother found him. No one could bring out the strained tone in her voice like his father.

"What is it?" Her distress saddened him, and yet part of him did not want to know what his father had done this time.

"He's over there with the horses."

Duncan nodded. "I saw him earlier."

"He's been betting. I asked him where he got

money to gamble, when we barely had enough for the rent."

Blood drained from Duncan's face. "And his answer?"

She met his gaze with regret. "He's lost almost all of it."

He asked knowing the answer, but not wanting to believe it. "My money? But I hid it."

"He's clever when it has to do with whisky or gambling. He must have watched you put it there. There's no other explanation."

Duncan cursed, and then said he was sorry for cursing.

She went on. "He must have seen you hide it, or discovered it."

It was all he could do to hold back his rage. He had saved money while he was gone so they would not have to worry, come rent time. He had taken jobs sailing to make even more. After a lifetime of struggles, he could not stand to be without money enough to feel safe and secure. Since Duncan was old enough, he had worked the farm while his mother made extra money selling baked goods and knitting to sell at the mercat. They had always gotten by, but just barely. For all of his faults, Duncan had always thought his father to be an honest man. Now he would have to add thievery to his father's list of fine traits. Duncan slowed his pace to match his mother's, elsewise he would have been at a full run toward the horse races to confront his father. It was better this way, at least for his father, to have time to tamp down his fury.

Brodie did not see his son coming as Duncan

clapped a firm hand on his shoulder and spun him around. "Where's the rent money?"

His father's helpless mien fed Duncan's anger.

"What is left? Give it to me."

Brodie dug into his sporran and pulled out a couple of coins, which he put in Duncan's outstretched hand.

"Is that all?" Duncan asked.

The answer was the same sheepish expression Duncan had seen too many times.

"You stole from me, Da."

When he would not look him in the eye, Duncan clutched Brodie's shoulders and shook him. "Why did you do it?" When no answer came, Duncan tightened his grip on his father's shirt collar.

"I'm sorry, lad. I was going to make us enough to get us all through the winter."

"Duncan, stop!" Elspeth grasped Duncan's arm. "You're making it worse."

Duncan obeyed his mother for her sake, but he glared at his father with contempt. "You're a poor excuse for a man." Duncan released his father. It threw Brodie off balance. He fell to the ground.

As she helped Brody to his feet, Elspeth quietly said, "Help me take him home."

Duncan's anger was slow to subside.

"Please, Duncan, help me." Elspeth took in the stares from onlookers.

Without a word, Duncan hooked his arms under his father's and pulled him to his feet.

"Come Brodie, it's time to go home," said his wife. She took one side, and Duncan took the other.

"I'm sorry," said Brodie.

Duncan cast a dark look at his father. "Try to walk
to those trees over there without disgracing your wife.
It's too late for me, but at least have a care for Mum."
He turned toward his mother. "Wait over there, out of
sight. I'll bring my horse, and he can ride while we
walk home the rest of the way."

As he walked past, people turned their attention
back to the horse race, but Duncan did not notice. His
mind was on how they would now pay the rent that
was due.

He had to walk past some overgrown brambles to
untether his horse. Muted moans caught his attention.
Thinking someone was hurt, he glanced toward the
sound.

With her palms to the tree, Rose's skirts were hiked
up, and a man gripped her hips. Her breasts slapped
against her ribs as he thrust himself into her. Rose
stared blankly ahead as the man lifted his chin to suck
in air and exhale. It was Tavish. Duncan turned away
and led his horse past groups of people dancing and
talking. Through the dancers, he caught glimpses of
Jenny on the opposite side. She was alone.

Chapter 6

A Walk in the Woods

DUNCAN'S FATHER LAY SNORING WHEN DUNCAN LEFT the next morning. On his way to the door, his mother awoke.

"Where are you going?" she asked.

"I've something to do." His terse answer discouraged further questions. At the door, Duncan turned back with a softening look. "Dinnae fash yersel, Mum. I'll take care of us."

He closed the door and started toward the byre, as he muttered, "But I dinnae know how."

A FEW MILES from the cottage, Duncan arrived at a burn with steep banks lush with foliage. He tethered his horse by the water and walked along the bank, soothed by the sound of rushing water. As a child, he had come here with his father. Brodie had told his young son that he came here for the aqua vitae, but the words meant nothing to young Duncan. All he cared about was the fun he had climbing the banks of the burn and playing pirate of the high seas. Large boulders were ships. He had many adventures while his father was busy. The tall trees lining the burn made for exciting adventures. Duncan paused to recall and then walked on, pulling branches out of his way.

Since he had returned, his father had disappeared during the days, and returned in his usual staggering condition. It was a familiar pattern, but now it would stop. Duncan spied a familiar tree and the rocks that had served as his ships. There it was. Inside the cave's entrance was the same old homemade distilling equipment: a brick still with a tube that led to a condenser. Attached to that was a pot to collect the distilled whisky. Behind that was a sight Duncan had not expected. In the back of the cave, there were dozens of barrels, each one marked with the date in black charcoal numbers. So this was what his father did instead of working the farm to ensure that his wife had a roof over her head and some food to eat. Duncan's first impulse was to take an axe to them. Since he did not have an axe, he picked up a barrel. It was heavy, but Duncan was strong and angry. At the mouth of the cave he heaved it onto a sharp-edged rock. Some splashed on him. He now smelled of whisky, but that was the least of his cares. Duncan sniffed the scent of smoked peat and oak from the barrels. His father might be a drunk, but he made a good whisky. His anger now spent, Duncan sat down not feeling nearly as satisfied from his anger as he had hoped. He could smash every one of the barrels, but he still had no money for rent. He had lost his love and would soon lose his home.

Duncan looked to the future, and it was bleak. He could get by on his own, but his father would be more of a burden than he was now. Most of all, he worried about his mother. The years with Brodie had been hard on her. She did not move without pain. How would she manage to wander from town to town on foot? They would need to find lodgings and money for food before the cold weather set in. But to do that, they would need work and wages. Duncan buried his face in his hands. "If bloody whisky were money, we'd be rich."

Duncan sat up straight and glanced back toward the cave. "But it could be." He got up and went to the broken pieces of barrel. A small bit of whisky was pooled in a curved wooden piece. Duncan lifted it to his lips for a taste. He looked back at the barrels. By the time he was finished counting them, a broad grin lit his face. "Well, Da, perhaps you're not entirely useless after all."

JENNY GLANCED BACK at her house to make sure no one would see, and then followed a footpath into the woods. It was shady and peaceful. A twig snapped and leaves rustled. Fearful, Jenny turned. "Duncan!" She smiled in relief, but he did not smile back.

"What are you doing here, Jenny?"

"I might ask the same."

"I was on my way home when I saw you."

Jenny hid her disappointment. She had thought he might have come here hoping to see her on the path they had so often walked together.

"It isnae safe nor right for a young lady to walk alone in the woods."

She could not disagree. All that she could offer was a weak defense. "I wanted some time to myself."

Duncan stiffened and gave a curt nod. "Aye, well I'm sorry I intruded." His voice dropped off at the end. Sorrow was the last thing he felt.

Realizing that he'd misunderstood her, Jenny reached out to touch his arm. "You are not intruding." He shot a look at her hand on his arm. Jenny pulled her hand back. She had touched him without thinking, as she once might have done. She went on talking to cover the tension between them. "I needed to get away from everyone at home. All they talk of is—" Jenny caught herself. He did not need to hear of the wedding.

Duncan watched her squirm. "Go on."

"It's blether." She could say nothing now to dispel the tension, so she exhaled and stared at the ground. In truth, she felt alone and adrift. Her once beloved home stifled her now that the wedding drew near. She had to get away so she could breathe. But she could not say that.

Duncan's tone softened. "May I help you with that?" Without waiting, he took her basket and gave a nod. "Shall we?" He smiled the same smile that had filled her with warmth for as long as she could remember. "It might help if you told me what we're looking for."

"Pine roots."

"Aye?" He nearly smiled. They were surrounded by pines.

"To burn as candles," said Jenny.

He smiled as he glanced about. "I suppose we might find one or two."

From there, they lapsed into the easy manner of past times. But as the basket grew full and the time came to part ways, they could no longer pretend things were as they used to be. They arrived near the edge of the woods and stopped.

"I should go home," Jenny said.

"Aye." Duncan took a step, but Jenny did not follow. "What is it?" asked Duncan.

Troubled, Jenny softly said, "I should go on alone." Her expression softened. "I'm sorry."

Duncan forced a smile. "No, you're right. We'd best not be seen walking together." Gently, he slipped the basket handle over her arm and let his hand linger with it for a moment. His fingers brushed the inside of her elbow.

Jenny looked at his hand, strong and marked with scratches and scars, some of which were new to her. She touched one gently.

A moan escaped. He tried to conceal it by clearing his throat, but the pain showed in his dark look, and it made her heart ache. The next instant, it was gone, his eyes blank. Jenny opened her mouth to say something. She did not know what.

Duncan looked at her parted lips. Abruptly, he turned and walked back into the woods. There he would wait, as he always had done, until he could emerge without anyone linking him with her.

Jenny walked home, her eyes shining with tears that she would not let spill. She had nearly told him the truth. Had she done so, she was sure that he would have swept her into his arms. He would have taken her back and thought later of how he would care for his parents. Jenny wished that he would, but she knew from having dreamt of it so many times, that it never could be. They might be happy for a time, but the burden of merely surviving would weigh them all down. Then the guilt would set in, and soon after, resentment. She always arrived at this impasse. It was hopeless unless she could persuade her father to change his mind.

JENNY STOOD outside the door to her father's study. She had postponed this all day, for she knew that it would not be easy. But there was nothing else to be done, so she took a deep, fortifying breath and walked in.

"Jenny?" He smiled, but his lined face looked strained. She could see that this was not a good time, but there never would be for what she had to say. She stepped inside and quietly spoke. "Father."

His quill remained poised in his hand as he stared expectantly at her.

With tentative steps, Jenny walked to the desk. She sat down across from him and thought through the words she had practiced. She recalled Duncan's face watching her dance with Tavish. Her betrayal had burned beneath his dark brow. She could no longer bear it.

"Jenny, if you've something to say, please be done with it. I'm busy, and haven't the time."

With a reflexive nod, she said, "Yes, well, the truth is..." Jenny paused. She should not have looked at him directly. With one glance, he reduced her to a timid young child. Jenny knew that he would. She had steeled herself for it, but beneath her strained confidence was a withering spirit. The strong declaration she had practiced came out as a muted woe. "I cannae do it."

"Do what," said her father, his mind elsewhere as he perused a few papers and then set them aside. With a sigh, he regarded her. "Cannae do what?"

"Marry Tavish." When he was silent, Jenny repeated, "I cannae marry Tavish. I dinnae love him."

"You'll not be the first to marry and fall in love later."

"No, but I cannae do it." Then it all spilled out. "I willnae marry him, father. I love someone else. I love Duncan. I always have, and I always will. And if you put Duncan's family out, I'll go with them, with Duncan, if he'll have me, which he may not after the pain I have caused him." Jenny glanced down at her trembling hands and then back at her father. She clung to what was left of her courage, and softly said, "Either way, whether Duncan forgives me or not, I cannae marry Tavish, for I dinnae love him, and I never will."

With complete attention, Andrew listened until she was finished. From his stern scrutiny rose an unsettling smirk. He got up and poured himself a glass of whisky.

When he returned, he sat on the edge of his desk, facing her with a chilling smile. "My dear girl, you have grown into a lovely young lady." With the pride of a father for his child, he lifted her chin and gazed. "But it's time to let go of your childish notions. You dinnae have to love him." His voice grew even quieter. "But you do have to marry him. And you will. I'll hear no more of it." With a kiss on the forehead, he took both her hands and drew her from her seat. "Come, let's see where your mother is."

Her protest came out almost as a whisper. "No." She paused in the doorway. "It's no use. I love Duncan, and I'm certain he loves me still."

He stiffened. When he turned to face her, he showed none of the anger that Jenny expected. All he offered was a cold stare.

"The matter is settled."

Jenny raised her voice. "No, it isnae. I cannae live without Duncan."

"Very well. If you must have him, be discreet about it. Go and roll in the hayricks with your cotter, but first you will marry Tavish MacLean."

"I couldnae marry Tavish and be Duncan's mistress."

Her father had a look in his eye she had never seen before. "You'd be surprised what you can do." Andrew turned and went back to his desk.

JENNY LEFT THE HOUSE. She could not bear to be in it or near anyone having to do with the wedding. Her father had never been unkind or harsh to her, so the thought of disobeying had never before crossed her mind. But she could not marry a man knowing that she loved another. Nor would she be anyone's mistress. Even as she told herself that she would not, she knew in her heart that she loved Duncan enough to do anything that she could to be with him. If their love had not changed, she would fight for it, no matter the cost. If being his mistress was all that she could have, she would be that, but she knew it would not be enough.

She had no time to spare. On the morrow, the banns would be called for the first time. She would find him and force him to listen to her. There was nothing else to be done but to tell him the truth. He would know what to do. Even if her father cast out Duncan's family, they would find a way to survive it together. They had to.

Jenny walked up to the door of Duncan's cottage and started to knock, but a sound from inside made her pause. Duncan's mother was crying. Jenny could guess at the cause. Elspeth had not drawn an easy lot in life, although few ever saw the burden she carried. Just yesterday, Elspeth had come out of the study and nearly collided with Jenny. Jenny had thought little of the muted apology when she had brushed past to slip out the door. But she must have been crying, as she was now. Jenny stared at the door. How many more tears would she shed after losing her home? Being with Duncan would come at a terrible cost. She should leave, she decided. With a turn, she found herself facing Duncan.

"Jenny?"

A sob from inside the cottage drew a dark glance from Duncan.

Jenny said, "This isnae a good time. I'm sorry." She started to brush past him, but he touched her shoulder to stop her. A rush of desire took her breath. From the way he pulled his hand back, Jenny saw that he felt it, too.

He glanced toward the door. "Come inside. It will lift her spirits to see you."

He reached past her to open the door, but Jenny touched his arm gently to stop him. "I came to see you." When she dared look up past his clenched jaw, sadness welled up within her.

"No," he said. "When I saw you earlier, I was reminded." His face nearly masked his emotions, but his fierce eyes betrayed him. He was as miserable as she.

"Reminded of what?" she asked, fearing the answer.

"Of how much we have lost." He clenched his jaw.

"Aye." Whatever else she might have said was caught in her throat.

"By your choice," said Duncan. His bitter glance pierced her. "I'll not deny my mother the company, for she loves you like a daughter." He stopped and swallowed. He shook his head, but could not speak until he looked away. "But dinnae come here to see me again. Ever." He turned and walked to the byre.

Jenny followed him. Inside the byre, Duncan busied himself to avoid her. When he could take no more, he stopped in his tracks with his back to her. "Why will you not go?"

"I cannae."

His stance softened, but he would not turn to face her.

A year's worth of longing and sorrow rushed to the surface. "Please, look at me, Duncan."

"Why?"

"So I can tell you I'm sorry."

"Are you?" A bitter laugh trailed off. "I am, too." He did, at last, turn with a blistering look.

Jenny flinched. "I had to do it for you."

"Did you, now? For me?" His eyes darted about as though searching for something.

Jenny mistook the quiet that followed for calm, until he turned his searing gaze to her and said, "I have despised you for months."

His words struck their target, but she could not blame him. He had every reason to hate her. She said softly, "I love you."

Without even a glance, he said, "I have seen love. For months, I watched Callum's Mari and saw what love was, and I knew then that I didnae have it. She loved him with a strength few men possess. And the more that I saw her, the more I knew that your love was false."

"Not false. I loved you."

"Once. But your love was weak. Worse–it was cruel."

"No. Dinnae say that."

"It was. Mari nearly lost Callum, but she never wavered an instant."

"Mari? What has Callum's Mari got to do with us?" Jenny stopped, stunned by the answer that came to her mind. "You loved her." She peered into his eyes. "You love her yet."

"Och! You're a fool! Can you not see that I love–" Duncan paused to measure his words. "That I...loved Mari's devotion to Callum, and the way that she cared for him–for us all. She was kind and good. Her heart was his, and it always will be."

"And what of your heart?"

"My heart? Before or after you pledged yourself to Tavish?"

"Why can I not make you understand?"

"You cannae make me do anything, Jenny, including not love you."

Her heart pounded as she whispered, "And I love you."

When he spoke, his deep voice was unnaturally calm. "Go home to your man."

"He's not my man."

"But he is. You are promised to him as you once were to me."

Jenny shut her eyes. A tear slipped free from her lashes. He reached out and touched her moist cheek with his thumb. If that had been an impulse or kindness, then holding his hand there was not.

"Jenny." His voice was fraught with both longing and anger.

Jenny leaned into the warmth of the palm of his hand where it lay on her cheek. Her lips parted at the base of his thumb. With that touch, Duncan flinched and pulled her to him. The kiss that came next was impulsive and greedy. She molded her body to his. It would not be enough.

His lips brushed hers as he murmured, "I hate you," and kissed her again.

Jenny clung to him as he clutched her against his hard body and caught the force of their weight with his hand as they slammed against the stall. Her breath quickened as Duncan yanked her skirts up by the handful and hoisted her legs up to circle his waist.

Jenny's hands ran freely over his powerful back and hard muscles. She could not reach him with words, but she would with her body. She had longed for the feel of his skin against hers. She would have him, no matter the cost, for her love had gone past reason or restraint. What once was shared joy now was anguish, but they were no longer apart. And so there, against the byre stall, they took what they could have of each other in desperate thrusts and forced exhalations until their bodies were spent. But their hearts would not be assuaged.

AFTERWARD, they were still. Duncan held her against him, as the sound of their breathing grew quiet.

"I love you," she said in a breathless whisper. "I've always loved you."

Duncan's voice faltered. "But you will marry him." He set her down and let go.

"I dinnae want to. I never did." Cold silence hung

between them. Jenny peered into his eyes. "My father arranged it."

He scoffed as he pulled his trews on and fastened them. "Do you think I dinnae know that? But you went along with it, when you should have said something."

"What was there to say?"

"No!" Duncan lowered his voice, but his anger still burned. "You could have said no."

"He left me no choice."

"There's always a choice."

"Is there? And what should I have done with you gone—set off on my own to search for you somewhere in the lowlands? And if I found you, what then?"

Softly, he said, "Then I would have married you."

"*Och*, Duncan, if you could know how I've dreamt of just that, but my father said—"

"I dinnae care what he said!" He pounded his fist on a plank of the stall, and it cracked. Duncan cursed and walked to the door and stared into the gloaming. "What does it matter?" He turned, eyes burning. "You'd rather lose me than stand up to him."

"No, that's not true." She took a step toward him, but he bristled. She stayed an arm's distance away.

Duncan ran his fingers through his hair. "This was a mistake."

Jenny took a sharp breath and stepped toward him. "No, dinnae say that."

"Stay away."

When she gingerly slipped her arm into his, he removed it and turned to her, gripping her shoulders. With a glance toward the stall, he said, "I wish that had never happened."

"No." It was a small, mournful sound.

"Don't you see? Nothing's changed."

"Not our love. That has never changed."

Duncan's eyes flared. "What of it? What do you want from me, Jenny?"

"I want you. I want us."

"We've lost us. You threw us away."

"Duncan, please." She reached out.

He took hold of her wrist with a warrior's grip.

Jenny tried to twist her hand loose. "My father told me I must, or—"

"And you are an obedient child," Duncan said with disdain. "You're too weak to honor our promise. No, Jenny. As long as you are betrothed, I'll not see you."

"You can't mean that." She searched his eyes, but found no love there.

"Dinnae touch me again." He released her with a force that threw her off balance. She staggered back a few steps to regain it. Raw pain broke through his words. "You think you can marry him and live in your grand house, then come back to me now and then when you're lonely?"

"No! I want what we had."

Duncan's wrath flared. "This isnae what we had. We're two people clutching at mist."

"No, we're more than that."

"'Tis not enough."

"Duncan, I love you."

"Your love is like you. It is weak and of no use to me."

Jenny could not react.

"Go home to your father and lie in the bed he has told you to make for yourself."

He left her in the byre, while the sound of his long strides echoed in her ears.

Chapter 7

The First Time of Asking

JENNY SAT IN THE KIRK THE NEXT MORNING, EYES DRY and swollen. She had cried herself to exhaustion. Rather than finding her way back to Duncan, she had driven him further away. If it was weakness that drove her once more to his arms, she did not regret it. It would be her last memory of him, to remind her that once he had loved her. She wondered now, even if he had given her chance to tell him the truth, would it have made any difference? Even as his rage left no room for forgiveness, Jenny's love was as boundless as the sorrow it brought her. What a great price to pay, only to wind up apart.

Here she was in the kirk. On one side was her family, on the other, Tavish and his parents–all happy, but Jenny. They had what they wanted.

The priest smiled at her as he called the banns for the first of three times before the wedding would take place. "If any of you know cause or just impediment why these persons should not be joined together in Holy Matrimony, ye are to declare it. This is for the first time of asking."

"Say something, Duncan," wished Jenny. She only looked back at him once. Dark eyes pierced her, but she could not react. All eyes were on her.

The priest finished, and the room seemed to sway like the deck of a ship. She was hot, and the air was too close.

Jenny turned to her parents. Her father may as well have been stone, for his eyes were as hard. She turned the other way to find Tavish peering at her with concern. Jenny put her hand to her temple in a failed effort to avoid his scrutiny.

When Mass ended, Tavish seemed to talk with everyone present. Jenny could not breathe. The damp stones in the walls seemed to thicken the air until panic rose within her. When Tavish turned to greet someone new, Jenny slipped away and rushed outside, where she came face-to-face with Duncan.

The heavy kirk doors opened. They glanced over to see people filtering outside. Duncan turned to leave, but Jenny reached out and put her hand on his forearm to stop him. "I did it for you. I had to–for your parents."

"What are you saying?"

She was making no sense, and she knew it. She had spoken on impulse. "I cannae do this."

Tavish emerged from the church and spied Jenny just as she withdrew her hand from Duncan's arm. Someone stopped Tavish to talk, but he kept a sharp eye on Jenny. There was so little time.

"Duncan, I cannae talk now. I wanted to tell you the truth last evening, but..." His eyes darkened at the memory. For the first time, his gaze settled on hers. Only hours before, they had been one in body and spirit. Their eyes locked until Tavish's voice carried to them.

Jenny glanced toward Tavish and then lowered her eyes and her voice. "I owe you the truth. Please meet me later."

"Dinnae play games with me, Jenny. I'm in no mood."

"Please, Duncan."

Duncan walked away just as Tavish strode over to clasp Jenny's hand. It was an act of possession, but the gesture was wasted on Duncan. He had already turned his back and joined his mother to escort her home, and he did not look back.

AFTER DINNER, Jenny complained of a headache and retreated to her room, leaving Tavish to play chess with her father. Minutes later, the cook glanced up to see Jenny at the foot of the stairs. She held a finger up to her lips. With a sharp eye toward the inside hall door, the cook shook her head, but turned away to continue her chores in tacit approval as Jenny slipped out through the back door.

When she was safely out of view, she began to have doubts. Was she letting desire outweigh her reason? She certainly had when she threw herself at him the day before. There was no other way to describe it. But for all it had cost her, that moment in his arms was worth the world to her. Pressed against his strong chest, she had breathed in his scent, and melted into his embrace. When he held her, she felt close to the place in his soul where no one else could be. In that moment, they had not forgotten their wounds, but their need for each other was greater.

The price for that moment was to be pierced by the words she would never forget.

"Your love is like you. It is weak and of no use to me."

A THICK MIST rolled in and brought with it the scent of fresh rain. As Duncan rode down the path toward the woods, a dark form crossed before him in the mist. He reined in his horse just in time to avoid her. He quickly dismounted and grabbed hold of Jenny's shoulders. "Did you nae hear me coming?"

"I thought you saw me."

"Are you daft? Look about you."

"I'm sorry."

"Never mind, lass. 'Tis my fault. I was riding too fast."

"I wasnae sure if you'd come," Jenny said as they walked into the woods.

"Nor was I," he said grimly as he tethered his horse to a sturdy branch. "Out with it, lass. What would you tell me?"

"It's about your parents."

Duncan shot a sharp questioning look at her.

Jenny met his eyes squarely. "After you left for the fighting, Tavish and his parents came visiting."

"Aye, he came later. I only remember because, when he caught up to us, he was boasting about his betrothal. We were all congratulating him. Then he said it was you, and I wanted to shove his words back down his throat and his face with it."

His eyes narrowed with fresh anger as he recalled it. Jenny put a gentle hand to his shoulder, but he shrugged it off so violently that she took a step back.

Duncan tamped down his emotions.

"I refused," Jenny said.

"Well you did a poor job of it." He looked over his shoulder.

"I said no to my father. Do you know how hard that was for me?"

"I know that you're scared of him. You have been since you were a wee girl. But God's wounds, Jenny, you're a woman full grown. And you'd already promised yourself to me."

"I know, but—"

"No, Jenny! We both made a promise! And one of us kept it." He turned away, keeping his anger in check. After a long pause, his breathing grew steady and calm.

Jenny said, "My father said he would evict your parents."

Duncan whipped about to face her. It could not be true.

She went on. "If I didnae agree to wed Tavish, he would have evicted them."

"He couldnae have. Everyone would have despised him."

"But he would have done, just the same."

"So you agreed to the marriage—"

"For you. And for your parents."

Jenny's words gripped his heart. "But why was he so keen on Tavish for you that he'd do such a thing?"

"Such things are done all the time."

"And he forced you to keep silent." Duncan thought of the pain she had suffered for more than a year. Jenny had done it for him. In return he had scorned her. All the while, she had carried this secret.

Duncan thought back on his last night before leaving. "Tavish stood beside you on our last night together."

"But I was with you."

Duncan said, "Before that. It is why I missed my footing and touched the sword during the dance. I was watching the two of you."

Jenny said, "I'd forgotten. He said he had something to tell me, but insisted that we be alone. I told him I was watching the dancing, so he said he'd wait. I slipped away to meet you."

"So he stayed a day later to do it, did he not? But by then, you were promised to me. You should have stood up to your father and told him."

"I told him about us and that we were promised. But he said that there were no witnesses, so there was no proof."

"Just a vow before God." Duncan's gaze bore through her.

"I tried to argue with him, but he wouldnae be moved. You were not there to help your parents, and Tavish was leaving."

"So you were promised to two men, and both of us gone."

Duncan took Jenny's hand in his hands. "Our vow shouldnae have been broken."

"I was never going to marry Tavish. You know I could not. So I did what would keep your parents safe in their home. I thought that when you came home, we would sort it all out."

"Sort it out? You were mine. I was yours. A hand-fast is as good as a marriage."

"For a year and a day."

Duncan looked as though the wind had been knocked out of him.

Jenny put words to Duncan's reaction. In a soft voice, she said, "You were gone longer."

"Hearts do not know the law."

"Nor can they fight against it." Jenny drew closer to Duncan.

He reached out his hand to stop her, but the touch of her hand on her shoulder softened his hardened expression. He let himself gaze at her. "For more than a year I believed that you wanted to wed that rogue."

"What else could I do? Send a letter with Tavish?"

Duncan shook his head. She was right.

Jenny said, "There was nothing I could do but wait until you returned."

"And what if I had not come home?"

Jenny lifted soft blue eyes to meet his. "Then I

would have lost my true love." She touched his face tenderly. "And your parents would still have had a home."

"But when I came home, you did nothing. Why did you not tell me?"

"I was going to, but then I heard how far behind you were with the rent."

Duncan fought back his resentment. "My da took the money I'd saved, and he lost it all gambling."

"You needed some time before being forced to move out."

"Could you nae have told me the truth while I saved up the money?"

"And what would you have done—come to steal me away?"

"Aye, it sounds like a very good plan." Duncan fought a smile.

"Do you know how I've wished for just that? But it wouldnae have helped you. Not then." Her soft gaze found his dark eyes and the regret that was etched there. After more than a year, Jenny had thought through it all. She had done what was best for his family, but at what cost to them both?

"My darlin'." Duncan held Jenny close. "I'd have gone to your father to plead for your hand."

"I know."

Overcome with anger toward Tavish, Jenny's father, his own, and most of all, himself, Duncan stared at the castle. He had let Jenny down, forced her to carry a burden that he should have born, but could not.

"We must end it now. I must go to your father and ask for your hand."

"He will say no, and you know it."

"But I owe him that much. It's a matter of honor." Duncan grinned. "Stealing his daughter isnae, but I'm willing to let go of that bit of honor, just once."

"Duncan, I've seen his ledger. Your rent is over a year past due. How can you support us all now?"

He clenched his jaw. "Thanks to my father, not as well as before. But I've found a new source of income."

"Have you taken to highway robbery now?"

"No, but I've found my father's whisky. It brings a good price in the cities. But I'll need a few more trips to sell it all."

With a deep, hopeless sigh, Duncan said, "In the meantime, you're still yoked to Tavish." His eyes darkened.

"I will wait until you are ready," she said.

"You cannae wait for long. They're already calling the banns."

"You'll not let me marry him, will you?"

With a warm smile, Duncan said, "No, I promise you that." For months, he had hidden his feelings behind dark, stormy eyes. With a guttural sigh, he pulled her to his chest. "You're my Jenny, and I'll not let him have you."

Jenny said, "You fair broke my heart every time I saw the betrayal in your eyes."

He took held her gentle face in his battle-scarred hands. "And what do you see now?"

"I see how you once looked at me."

"How I loved you?"

"And how you let me love you."

He leaned down and kissed her. The full lips she had longed for were hers. She was in his embrace. His body against hers was home. Together at last, they found peace from the yearning that had haunted them for so long.

Duncan lifted and carried her to the base of the tree, where he set her down gently on a blanket of leaves. There he slowly undressed her. He touched her with his hands and his lips, and his fingers stroked the soft places he had once tried to forget. Her sighs in his ears fueled the need to be part of her. Jenny wanted him, too. Her hands sought him through the thick woolen trews to the point of near torture. With fevered impatience, he freed himself of them, kicking them free of his ankles as he lowered himself to her. He could not let her know how helpless he was in her arms. At the same time, he felt fiercely protective. Jenny MacRuer was his for as long as she would have him, and no other man would get near enough to hurt the woman he loved. And Duncan was hers, as he always had been. Woe to any who dared try to part them again.

DUSK SETTLED about them as Duncan lay beside Jenny and watched as she sighed, eyes closed and content. A gentle smile formed on his lips as he stroked away soft strands of hair from her brow. She tilted her head until her lips found his.

"We will have to leave soon," she said, laying her cheek on his shoulder.

"Aye, and I will let you go–for today."

"And tomorrow?" asked Jenny.

"I will find a way. I cannae live without you."

"What if there is no way?"

"You are mine, and I am yours. I'll not let you go."

Chapter 8

A Man of His Word

IT WAS NEARLY DARK WHEN JENNY CREPT INSIDE through the kitchen door. "Where have you been?" said her father in a stern, but hushed voice.

Jenny flinched. "Walking."

His eyes narrowed. "Walking? So your headache is better."

Jenny had nearly forgotten. "My headache? Oh yes, the fresh air—"

"Come with me." They would not talk in the kitchen, where the household staff might overhear. With a firm grip on her elbow, Andrew led his daughter to his study. As soon as he closed the door behind him, Andrew's face reddened. "Dinnae lie to me, lass, for I know where you've been and with whom!"

Jenny flinched. Even fiercer than his words was the condemnation. As Jenny took in a breath, bracing herself to deny it, Tavish rose from a chair in the corner. She had not noticed him there, as had no doubt been his intention. Jenny turned to her father, but found no quarter there. She exhaled and cast her eyes downward. "I've done nothing wrong."

Andrew yelled, "Dinnae lower yourself even more by denying it!"

Her cheeks flushed as her father proceeded.

"You were seen with that cotter."

Jenny lifted her chin, wanting to seem bold, but soon withered. She hated herself for it.

Tavish rescued her from the tense silence. "Sir, might I speak with your daughter alone?"

Andrew MacRuer cast a questioning look at Tavish, who appeared the most calm of the three. As the wronged party, he clearly had the advantage, which he now gently pressed. He was all grace and forgiveness, which Jenny found hard to believe. With a gruff nod, her father retreated, closing the door firmly behind him. Tavish offered his arm. "Will you come to the window, Jenny? Look at the sunset. It's very pretty." Tavish laid his hand upon hers, still linked in his arm. He gazed down at their hands as he stroked hers. "When I look to the sky in the evening, I expect some show of beauty. It doesnae disappoint."

Jenny wanted to run toward that sunset.

Still stroking her hand, Tavish spoke in soothing tones. "When I asked for this hand, I expected certain things."

Jenny braced herself, but with no warning, her guilt and her shame seemed to dissolve, as relief took its place. For she realized that after this, he would want to break off the betrothal. A scandal would follow, and yet all she could think of was how she would be free. She and Duncan could marry. Nothing else mattered. No matter what happened, she and Duncan would follow their hearts.

Tavish said, "The world is a very small place, and we are such a small part of it, really."

"Tavish, I'm sorry. I never wanted to hurt you."

"Hurt? No. But I was disappointed. I must say, though, you surprised me. You've got passion within that cold breast."

Now uneasy, her heart pounded as Tavish continued. "Aye, I saw your wee roll in the hay. Or should I say, in the leaves?"

Jenny could not form the right words to say.

Tavish watched her, amused. "I grew bored with your father's company, so I thought I'd go for a walk. When I reached the lane, I saw my sweet betrothed rushing into the woods with a man. So I followed you— for your protection." With a knowing gaze, Tavish smiled.

Jenny cringed.

"You are lucky I didnae tell your father all that I saw."

Dread weighed on her chest at the thought of her father's reaction.

"I told him a bit of a lie. I said you were out walking and holding your farmer boy's hand." He drew so close she could smell his warm breath. "I didnae tell him what else you were holding."

Nausea swept over her in a wave.

Tavish drew close until his lips nearly touched her earlobe. "My, my, Jenny. I find myself looking forward to our wedding night, and many nights after that." With a glance toward the door that Andrew had closed behind him, Tavish circled part way around Jenny until he faced the door. Taking hold of her shoulders, he planted a kiss on her forehead as his palms slid from her shoulders to her breasts.

Jenny pulled away, and spun about. "Touch me again, and I'll scream. Do you think we could marry after this?" She moved toward the door to put distance between them, but he grasped her hand firmly.

"But why not, my love?"

"I'm not your love, and you know it."

"But we're promised to one another."

"It was a mistake." She took a halting breath as she tried to steady her voice. "My father forced this upon me. It was not fair to you, and I'm sorry for that, but I cannae marry you."

"But you will." His confidence galled her.

"No, I willnae. I do not love you."

His eyes smoldered. "You are young and know little of men. These childish dreams of romance will wane. You will grow used to me. I dinnae care about love. But I expect you to make a good show of it." He lifted both her hands to his lips and kissed them. "Now, there's a good girl. Sit down while I go fetch your father to tell him we've patched up our wee misunderstanding."

He strode halfway across the room as Jenny said, "Did you nae hear me? I cannae marry you."

Tavish paused for a moment, teeth clenched, and then took his time walking back to her, being careful to maintain the appearance of propriety, lest anyone watch through the windows. He drew so close that Jenny reached her palms out to force distance between them, but he gripped her wrists drew them close to his chest. From afar, nothing would appear amiss. He spoke under his breath. "Unless you want me to tell your father what I saw in the woods, I would keep that mouth closed, my wee whore."

Jenny pulled her arm back to slap him, but his grip was too tight. Her cheeks burned. "If that's what you think of me, then release me."

"But my sweet wife to be, I find that I want you even more, now that I know you've a fire in your hearth."

His eyes swept down her body. "And besides, I'm a man of my word."

Jenny met his lie with helpless contempt. She could not let this happen. But, for now, she saw no way out.

With the crooked smile of a victor, Tavish abruptly walked out of the room.

"He's not here, lass." Duncan's mother stood in the cottage doorway, and smoothed back a stray curl. "Won't you come in? I've some fine tea that Duncan brought home for me. I've been waiting for good company to share it with."

Jenny forced a weak smile and went inside. She sat down as she had many times before, but this time without ease.

"*Och*, I'm out of water."

Before Elspeth had a chance to ask, Jenny rose. "I'll

fetch some." She scooped up the pail and was gone. Once outside, she saw him round the corner. "Duncan!" She ran after, but it was Charlie who turned around, grinning. "No, dearie. 'Tis your lucky day. You've found me instead."

"Charlie, what are you doing here?"

"That's a fine greeting," Charlie said with a glint in his eye.

"I'm sorry. I was looking for Duncan."

"So I gathered," Charlie said, with his most charming look of regret. "I'll have to do."

In no mood for his harmless flirtation, Jenny said, "Charlie. Where is he?"

"I'm afraid he's not here."

"I can see that. But where is he?"

A voice called out from the byre. "Charlie, you lout, will you come here to help me? I cannae wait all day." Alex emerged from the byre with a pitchfork in hand.

"Jenny, hello! Come to visit us, have you?" he said, knowing full well she had not, but as cheerful as if he had expected her visit.

Their easy manner made Jenny impatient. "Alex, where is Duncan? I must see him."

Alex reached for Jenny's pail. "Here, let me help you with that." The three walked toward the byre. "He left this morning for Inverlochy. He was in quite a hurry."

"Aye, he woke me out of a sound sleep," Charlie said.

Distressed, Jenny cut him off. "Whatever for? He said nothing to me."

That caught Charlie's attention. "Why should he tell you?"

Jenny looked away and thought quickly. He did not know that she and Duncan had been together. But how could she find out what she needed to know without rousing curiosity.

Charlie said, "He's been selling his father's whisky to pay off his debt to your father." Alex shot a sharp look, prompting Charlie to mumble the end of the sentence.

Jenny frowned at the thought of what Duncan had gone through because of her father and his.

Seeing her worried expression, Alex said, "Charlie, you'd be of more use finishing up in the byre."

"I'm of use wherever I am." Charlie smirked, but a glare from Alex put an end to it. "Ah well, I should get back now. I've got something important to do." He muttered to himself as he left them. "I dinnae know what it is, but as soon as I do, I'll tell you. I'm sure you'll be eager to hear it."

Alex waited until Charlie was far enough away not to hear. "I know about you and Duncan. He told me."

"And Charlie?"

"No, although he's no fool. He likely suspects."

Jenny shrugged. "'Tis of no matter now. My father knows. We only kept it from you because you would tease us without mercy. There's no fun in that now." Jenny gazed into the distance. Her thoughts were with Duncan. "Inverlochy?" She said it more to herself than to Alex.

Alex said gently, "He wishes to pay off his debt. I am sure he didnae wish to trouble you with it."

"When will he be back?"

"Soon enough."

"No, he won't."

That caught Alex off guard. "Why?"

"When did he say he'd return?"

Alex shrugged. "When he's sold his cartload of whisky."

Jenny held back her impatience. "How long will that take?"

"I dinnae know. If he sells it quickly, he'll return with an empty cart. Even so, a horse needs to rest on the way." Alex shrugged. "A bit more than a day?" He peered at her. "You're fair shaking. What is it, hen?" With a light touch to her elbow, he said, "Here, sit down."

"On the ground?"

Alex grinned. "Aye, 'tis good ground, and it's solid–unlike your legs, at the moment."

Jenny did as he told her. She peered at the dark clouds. "What has Duncan told you?"

Alex hesitated. "That he loves you."

"I love him, too."

"But you're marrying Tavish."

"I never meant to."

Alex leveled a knowing look at her. "Getting married is rarely an accident."

Jenny heaved an impatient sigh. "I had to let them believe I'd agreed until Duncan came home."

Alex said, "It's a dangerous game you are playing."

"I was forced."

"Forced?" Alex turned to her angrily. "Lass, has he hurt you?"

Jenny shook her head. "Not Tavish. My father. He arranged it. He left me with no choice."

Alex studied her.

Jenny looked at him. "Marriages are arranged all the time. You think little of it until it happens to you." She gave him a moment to consider her plight. "You will think me a terrible wanton." She forced the rest out. "Yesterday, Tavish saw me with Duncan. We were…together. Alone."

Alex peered at her, his question unvoiced.

"It is just as you're thinking." Before Alex had a chance to react, Jenny continued. "Tavish went straight to my father, and now they have moved up the wedding."

Alex opened his mouth, but before he could speak, Jenny said, "I'm to be married tomorrow!"

"Duncan will never stand for it."

"Nor will I, which is why I must go to him."

"'Tis out of the question. Even if you knew where he was, you're in no position to make such a trip."

"But I must."

"Your father will have Duncan's head on a pike."

"Not if Duncan takes me away with him."

"And his parents? Or have you forgotten about them?"

"They can come with us."

"And how will you live? Do you not know that the money is gone? His father gambled it all away." Alex put his hand on hers. "Lass, this is a battle that no one can win."

"No, you're wrong."

Alex had nothing to offer but sympathy.

"I'll not lose him, Alex." As determined as she was, tears welled up in her eyes to betray her own doubts.

Alex pulled her into comforting arms. "Lass, your plan cannae work, and you know it." He caught her fist before it could land on his chest. He winced, half amused through his pity. "Beating me willnae help it, hen."

Jenny had never felt anger like this, let alone expressed it. She had been an obedient child, and behaved like a proper young lady. No one was more surprised than she that she had lost her control. "I'm sorry! Alex, I dinnae know what I'm doing." She glanced about as though she might find the answers. "I've got to do something. But Duncan is so far away." Jenny got up. "I've no choice. I must go. I must go to him now."

"Jenny..." Alex stood up beside her.

"Even if I cannae find him, at least I willnae be married." Jenny gazed in the direction of Inverlochy.

He watched her, full of thoughts of his own.

Jenny turned to him. "What roads do I take? I'll need a horse. May I borrow a horse? If I take one of ours, my father will find out. I've saved up some coins. I can pay you."

"Do you not think your father will notice you've gone?" Alex said, with a skeptical glance from beneath his brow.

"Aye, but by the time he finds out, I'll have had enough time to get to Inverlochy before anyone can catch up." She went on, more to herself than to Alex. "If I borrow a horse and tether it nearby, I could sneak out after dark."

"Jenny." He was quiet at first, but she did not react. "Jenny!" He gripped her shoulders. "You are not going to Inverlochy."

Jenny looked up, transformed. With eyes bright with resolve, she said, "Oh, but I am."

Alex shook his head, unconvinced. "You'll have half the clan coming after you, and when they catch up to you—which willnae be long, assuming you haven't got yourself lost—I wouldnae put it past your father to have a priest with him to marry you to Tavish right on the spot. And you'd better hope that he finds you before you get to Duncan, because if Duncan is with you, he'll show the poor lad no mercy. And after that, his parents will surely be ousted from their wee cozy cottage, all helpless with no place to go."

Jenny exhaled, defeated. "Without Duncan, I'm helpless."

Alex touched her chin. "You're stronger than you think."

Jenny lifted doubtful eyes. "Am I?"

"Aye, and you must be strong now."

"Alex, you know me. I have never been strong. It has always been easier for me to yield—especially to my father. Until now, nothing mattered to me enough to confront him."

"And now?"

"And now, they've moved up the wedding—"

Alex nodded. "Because Tavish saw you with Duncan."

Jenny blushed. "I told you that. Must we dwell on it?"

"If we're to understand and decide what to do."

"There is naught to understand."

Alex barely heard her. "Why would Tavish still want to wed you?"

His words hurt her pride. "Because he loves me?"

"Knowing Tavish, I doubt it."

Jenny took exception to that. "Perhaps he forgives me?"

"He's a proud man. Some might even call him an arrogant, self-serving prig. But forgiveness?" Alex shook his head.

Jenny said, "What is it, then? What are you thinking?"

"'Tis not that a man couldnae love you, bonnie lass, but this man has no heart."

"'Tis no matter to me. I dinnae want his heart–or any part of him."

"But he wants something from you. Is it money?"

"He doesnae need my money."

"Or so he might have us believe," Alex said to himself.

Her thoughts turned back to what mattered most. "What am I to do if I cannae go to Duncan?"

Alex diverted his eyes as he shook his head. "Be practical, Jenny. How can you?"

"Because I can do nothing else."

The longer it took for him to respond, the less hope Jenny held, until, crestfallen, she pleaded. "Would you sentence me to wed Tavish?"

"I would never choose him for you."

"Nor did I."

"I'm sorry, lass, but I'll not send you off to the world unattended."

Jenny's face lit with a small bit of hope. "Then go with me." She put her hand on his arm. "Please, for Duncan."

With a kind look, Alex said, "Jenny, I cannae steal you away from your home."

"Yes, you can."

Alex smiled. "It is enough that you were discovered with Duncan. If I, yet another man, stole you away, you would shame yourself and your family—"

"I dinnae care about any of that."

Gently, he added, "And my family, as well. You may think that your father deserves what he gets, but my family doesnae. I cannae do this to them."

Jenny nodded. "You're right, of course. I've been selfish."

"No, lass." Alex took both of her hands in his. "I will help you and Duncan, but we must find another way. For now, I would keep you right here where you're safe."

"Safe? Safely married, you mean."

He peered into her eyes. "Do you trust me?"

"I am not sure," she said skeptically. "Should I?"

Alex smiled. "Not as a rule." His smile faded. "But in this case, you must. I will go and fetch Duncan to bring him back to you. If he chooses to run away with you, we'll have time to think through how best to do it. I promise to do all I can to help you both."

Jenny threw her arms around Alex's neck. He could not help but return her embrace, until he heard Charlie clear his throat loudly.

"Mrs. MacDonell was asking about the water." Charlie eyed the empty pail in Alex's hand, and then studied Alex. "Do you mind if I ask what you two have been doing?"

Jenny laughed lightly. "Alex has been making me very happy."

Charlie raised an eyebrow.

Chapter 9

A Proper Wedding

ALEX AND CHARLIE RODE AWAY TO MEET DUNCAN. With any luck, he would be on his way home. He had orders for most of his cartload of whisky, but took extra in hope of selling more. He needed to make enough to pay the rest of the past due rent, with some left over to begin a new life with Jenny. He had learned the hard way not to hide money at home. All of his savings were now stowed safely in Callum's home. Alex had traveled with Duncan before on one of his whisky-selling trips. If this trip went as well as the others, they could be back by Monday midday, only hours before the wedding was set to take place. He was not one to worry, but even Alex had doubts as to whether this plan would work.

On their second day of riding through heavy rain, both plaids and spirits were dampened. The weather had slowed down their progress. Charlie was first to say what they had both been thinking. "Have you thought about what we will do if we don't find Duncan?"

"I am not in the mood for your blether!" snapped Alex.

Charlie shrugged. "It wouldnae hurt to think ahead, just in case your plan doesnae work out."

"*Och*, now there's a fine idea. Let us make ourselves mad thinking of what could go wrong when we don't know when or where, or even how we will meet up with Duncan."

With a weary glance, Charlie turned and smirked. "Aye, well then, let us try to think of what could go right. Let us think...hmm..."

"To begin with, you could shut your flapping mouth, you clotpole."

Charlie reached over grabbed Alex. Just as he was about to unhorse him, Duncan called out.

The two released their grip one another with a slight shove on Charlie's part.

Duncan joined them, alarmed. "What is it? My parents? Has Jenny been hurt?"

"Nay, but if we dinnae hurry, you'll be addressing her as Mrs. Tavish MacLean," said Charlie.

Alex, still angry with Charlie, rolled his eyes. "Clumsily put, but 'tis so."

"But the wedding was not until tomorrow."

"It was until Tavish saw you with Jenny."

"God's teeth. Saw us where?"

Alex gave a somber nod, confirming the worst.

"It will take more than God's teeth to help you out of this one," Charlie muttered.

Alex gave Charlie a swat on the arm with the back of his hand.

Duncan, too preoccupied to notice, said, "But then, surely he broke off the betrothal."

"I wish I could say it was so," answered Alex. Gravely, he added, "But he is determined to marry the lass."

Charlie said, "Let us ride as we talk. Every moment will count."

The two others agreed. Charlie said, "Duncan, leave the cart here."

Alex surprised himself by agreeing. "We can come back for it later."

They concealed the cart behind some brambles, and Duncan mounted his horse. The three rode as fast as the rain and the rough road allowed, but the horses needed water and rest, so they stopped on the way.

"She could have been married by now."

Alex nodded. "Had they had a priest there, they would have been. To your good fortune, Jenny's father had to send someone to fetch one."

"But this happened—"

"Thursday," said Charlie.

Duncan's dark eyes clouded. "But it's Saturday. How far away can the nearest priest be?"

"Let us hope that he was farther than you were." Alex met Duncan's eyes frankly. "I made a promise to Jenny that we'd bring you back to her, and that we will do."

JENNY STOOD at the door to the chapel. Her father's stern look and firm grip propelled her down the short aisle toward the priest and, beside him, Tavish. He watched her with barely checked longing as her last step brought her to his side. His was not the smile of a man for the woman he loved. It was desire to complete the purchase of a coveted possession. With smoldering eyes, he surveyed her. A warm glow of triumph shone through his half grin. Some would mistake it for adoration. He turned to the priest, who appeared a bit worse for wear, and not only from travel.

The priest squinted and swayed just a bit, but enough to draw a bitter glare from Tavish. "God's teeth, you're three sheets to the wind. Where did they find you, holding mass in a tavern?"

The priest shot a cold look at Tavish, but gave up the thought as his stomach nearly got the better of him.

Tavish spoke through his teeth. "Well? Get on with it, father!"

The priest swallowed and steadied himself. Jenny barely heard the priest's voice as she listened for horses outside. There were none. Soon the time to exchange vows would come. She would have to wed Tavish. Everything that she loved about life would be gone.

They knelt at the altar. The hilt of Tavish's sgian dubh touched the floor. The quiet clink of metal to stone startled Jenny. The priest cleared his throat and continued. Jenny faced him obediently. Where was Duncan? Her whole life had led her to this point. She had always done what she was told, and this was her reward. She would be forced to wed a man whom she loathed.

Tavish moved. It was time to stand up. Jenny did, but as she rose she slipped Tavish's sgian dubh from the sheath on his stocking. Jenny took a step back and threatened Tavish with the scallop-edged blade.

The guests gasped.

"I'll not wed you! I'm sorry. I cannae," Jenny said, inching away from her groom.

"Jenny!" Her father stepped toward her, but Jenny took another step back. "Nay, I willnae. I tried to tell you, but no one would listen."

"Girl, dinnae be a fool." Tavish stepped toward her and reached for the sgian dubh, but as she evaded his grasp, the blade sliced into Tavish's hand.

"God's blood, you've cut me!" With the back of his good hand, he struck her across the face. The force of the blow knocked her down to her knees. She lost her grip on the sgian dubh, but she scooped it up and said, "If you touch me again, I will cut you again!"

With one swift motion, he kicked the knife out of her hand. Jenny scrambled for it, but Tavish put his boot on her wrist. She was hopelessly pinned to the floor as she struggled beneath his foot. Tavish grinned and said through his teeth, "My love's a wild beastie." He reached down and grabbed hold of her arms and pulled her to her feet. With his arms clamped about her waist, he barked for the priest to go on.

The priest said softly, "If the bride isnae willing, perhaps—"

"Hold your tongue. The sooner you finish, the

sooner you can get back to the flask you've got tucked in your robe."

The words struck their target. Humiliated, the priest cast his eyes down to escape Tavish's menacing scowl. He meekly resumed his recitation.

The oak doors to the chapel swung open as three swordsmen took command of the chapel. Tavish glanced back, and then said to the priest, "Go on!"

Duncan's voice rang through the chapel. "It cannae go on, for the lady is already married." Alex and Charlie each took a side at the rear of the chapel.

When Jenny's eyes widened, Duncan's dark eyes warmed her. "Have you not spoken vows before?"

Stunned as she was, her eyes shone. "Yes, I have."

Jenny's father spoke up. "If this is that handfasting nonsense, you've no proof that it happened."

"But it did," Duncan said. "I was a fool to let this go on for so long."

"Go now, lad." Andrew stood tall with a resolute gaze. "Or, by my troth, I will cast you and you parents from your home."

"I will take care of my parents." Duncan tamped down his anger.

Andrew said, "Go and take care of them now, for I'll not give you my daughter—handfast or not."

Ignoring Andrew, Duncan strode over to Tavish. "Release her."

Tavish laughed. "The devil take you and your handfast. I'll not let her go."

Some wedding guests gasped. The priest said, "You cannae speak like that in Lord's house."

Tavish let his smug smile descend upon the priest.

"And yet I just did." The smiled quickly faded to a weary gaze. "Now, pronounce us wed and be done with it."

In a quiet voice, the priest said, "But the vows must be spoken."

Tavish had just raised a brow and taken a breath to reply, when Duncan interrupted him. "Jenny, I vow to be your husband. Do you vow to be my wife?"

Jenny said, "I do."

Duncan smiled, "There. The vows have been spoken. If the handfast was not enough, we've now spoken our vows before a priest and witnesses. So that makes us married. Does it not, father?"

Slack jawed, the priest said, "Well, it is highly irregular."

"But is it legal?" Duncan waited, confident of the answer.

The priest's eyes darted to Tavish, and then turned back to Duncan, brow raised. "Under the law…"

Tavish said, "The law? So you're a barrister, too?"

The priest turned away.

Duncan said, "He's not, but a man that I spoke to in Inverlochy was."

Alex spoke up. "I heard vows. Did you, Charlie?"

With a grin, Charlie answered. "I did. That makes twice they have spoken them."

Nodding, Alex said, "Aye, so it does."

"But the banns!" Andrew cried.

The priest said, "If I may, the kirk prefers them, but they are not required."

"*Och!* Have you all gone daft? This isnae a proper wedding!" Andrew looked about. Everyone was as astonished as he, except Jenny's mother, who stared at her hands as she hid a smile.

No one moved until Tavish turned back to the priest. "They cannae just say that they're wed."

The priest shrugged. "I usually play more of a part in a wedding, but these two have made a vow before God. I've no power to undo what has been done here.

"You cannae be serious!" Tavish cried out with disdain.

Duncan took a step closer, sword still drawn. "I am. And now, let her go before I prove to you how very serious I am."

Tavish eyed the sword, inches from his face. If he held onto Jenny, he could not fight Duncan. If he chose to release her to fight back, his sword hand was cut. Even on his best day, he was no match for Duncan. He glanced at the red stain that bled from his hand to Jenny's dress. Tavish lifted his chin and met Duncan's steely gaze. "No." With his good hand, he pulled a dagger from his belt and held it to Jenny's throat. With that Tavish fainted.

Duncan swept Jenny into his arms. "Darlin' Jenny, my wife."

Jenny stared. "Is it true?" She looked to the priest to confirm it.

With a gleam in his eye, the priest said, "It is if I say so."

Duncan kissed Jenny, and whisked her away down the aisle, stopping first to face Andrew. "Here's the money that's owed."

Andrew fumed. "If you think this absolves you, you're wrong."

"Sir, I am paying a debt, that is all. As for Jenny, I love her. I seek no absolution for that."

Jenny's mother stood and grasped Duncan's arm as he swept Jenny past. "Be good to our Jenny."

"She will be safe and cared for. I promise."

Rowena took Jenny's face in her hands, and kissed her on the forehead. "Now go! His wound isnae fatal, but his anger could be."

Alex and Charlie leaned against the door, grinning. Charlie said, "I suppose they'll be needing an escort."

They all ran to their horses. As they had done many times growing up, Jenny circled her arms about Duncan's waist, and away they rode into the crisp Highland wind.

Chapter 10

The Price of Whisky

CALLUM SLID HIS HANDS ALONG THE CARVED OAK ARMS of his chair and leaned back. "You stole a bride from her wedding?"

Charlie chimed in with a glint in his eye, "But he married her first."

Callum looked to Alex for confirmation, and received a wry nod.

Jenny slipped her hand into Duncan's and waited for Callum to speak.

As he stared at the fire, Mari handed some ale to him and winked. "Who would do such a thing—stealing a woman away from her family?"

He lifted dark eyes to meet Mari's. "That was different, and you know it."

"Callum, they're in love. Would you deny them?"

"No, Mari, I wouldnae. But this presents difficulties."

"Difficulties?" Duncan made no effort to hide his anger. "Watching the woman I love getting wed to another was a difficulty I chose not to suffer. And saving your arse from a shipwreck was a wee bit difficult for me, as well, but I did it."

Callum's anger was the quiet sort that brought a profound hush to the room. Softly, he said, "I havenae forgotten that I owe you my life. If you're asking for payment–"

The chair scraped the floor as Duncan rose to his feet, followed closely by Callum. The two stood face-to-face, barely checking their wrath. Alex drew closer to Duncan and put a hand on his shoulder. Duncan shook it off as he said to Callum, "I would never ask that, and you know it."

Callum's ill temper faded. "I do. As you should know that I would help you in any way that I can. At the moment, I dinnae know what that is, though. So let us see what's to be done, and we'll do it."

With a sharp nod, Duncan sat down. The tension in the room eased.

Callum said, "I was thinking aloud, that is all. Tavish willnae be pleased that you've stolen his bride."

Duncan sneered. "Nor was I when he stole mine."

"Aye, well, you kept that wee fact to yourselves." Callum turned to Jenny. "And what of your father? What will he do?"

Jenny said frankly, "I dinnae ken what he'll do, but he has threatened to throw Duncan's parents out of their cottage."

"Has he? And when was that?" Callum asked her.

"Months ago, when I told him I loved Duncan and wanted to spend my life with him. But he told me I had to agree or he'd cast Duncan's parents from their home."

"She kept silent for us," Duncan said.

Callum's eyes softened. "I see."

Jenny said, "I dinnae ken what else to do." Duncan turned, and she met his warm gaze.

Callum took note. "Duncan, your parents will need somewhere to live, then."

"They will."

Mari smiled gently as she recalled. "There's a croft by the sea. 'Tis a wee bit remote, but I once found it quite pleasing."

"Aye, so did I." With a gentle smile, Callum gazed at his wife. "It isnae mine to offer, but I know it isnae being used. I will speak to my father about it. Will that do for your parents?"

"It will." He swallowed back emotion. "Callum, I dinnae know how to thank you."

"You are my friend. There is no more to say."

Charlie asked Duncan, "Where will you two live?"

I suppose that we'll live in the croft with my parents."

Charlie grinned. "Well that sounds very snug."

With a glance, Duncan warned Charlie. "We'll manage." Turning to Callum, he said, "In truth, I dinnae know how they'd manage alone."

Jenny said, "They won't have to. I love Duncan's parents as if they were my own. We will all work together to make it our home."

Alex said, "We can build a new croft of your own close to theirs."

Duncan was stunned.

When he started to thank him, Alex said, "Wheesht! Would you nae do the same for any of us?"

"Well, aye. But–"

Alex broke in. "Of course you would."

Charlie said, "All I ask in return is a dram of your father's whisky at the end of the day."

"Now that is a brilliant idea," said Alex.

"Getting Charlie drunk?" said Duncan with a raised brow.

Alex said, "Your father's whisky sells well enough. Could you not learn to make it as he does?"

Duncan nodded. "I could." He turned to Callum. "If your father is willing, perhaps we could stay there and pay him in whisky."

"Callum said, "I dinnae see why he wouldnae. Your father makes a fine whisky. No doubt he and his guests would enjoy it."

"There. Then it's all settled, except for one thing." Mari put her hands on her hips. "Have you all forgotten something?"

She was met with blank stares.

"We've a wedding to celebrate! All of you, arise from your chairs. You, too, Jenny." Mari dragged them to the center of the floor. "Charlie, sing. Callum, go fetch everyone you can find to play music. I'll have a room made ready. Of course, you'll bide here." She looked at Duncan and Jenny. "Dinnae stand there like you've nothing to do. Let's have a merry dance."

Duncan smiled at his bride. "You heard her. Dinnae stand there, my Jenny. Make merry with me!" He pulled her into his arms and spun her about. After planting a kiss on her lips, the dancing began.

HOURS LATER, Duncan and Jenny went up to their room, leaving the music and laughter behind them. Duncan closed and bolted the door and pulled Jenny against his warm body. Jenny pressed her softness against him and buried her face in his neck and inhaled his scent. "We're married!"

"'Tis true. 'Though your parents may never forgive me, I am yours forever. Poor you!" Duncan laughed and scooped her up into his arms and walked to the bed. There he set her down gently and leaned over her. A deep look clouded his eyes.

"What is it?" said Jenny, alarmed.

"You're so bonnie, and I love you so."

Jenny reached up and brushed the hair from his face. Her eyes filled with mist, which she would not permit, so she grinned. "Come here, husband. You'll have to convince me."

He did his best to do just that, beginning with her soft lips and working his way down the curves in her neck. She inhaled as he unlaced the ties of her shift at the neckline and tugged at her bodice. He set her free from her clothing and found every inch of silk skin he had longed for.

Jenny slid her hands up Duncan's powerful legs. "Take off your trews. Let me feel you against me." He did, eager to pull away every garment.

He moaned in her ear. "How I've missed you."

Their breathing grew ragged as their bodies sought to be closer. Her legs wrapped about his and she moaned. With teasing touches and greedy clutching they sought to be one. Jenny cried out and Duncan covered her mouth with his palm to muffle the sound, as he buried the rest of her cries with a ravenous kiss. Jenny gripped him and hungrily pulled him close as he plunged further into her. Desperate panting gave way to bliss as they held on, reluctant to part. Together, tangled as one, they lay still but for their rising and lowering chests and the breathing that slowed as their hearts beat together.

DUNCAN LAY SLEEPING, his arm stretched across Jenny's waist. Jenny awoke. There was shouting downstairs. Had an argument broken out below? Footsteps bounded down the hall to their room.

"Duncan!" It was Alex.

Jenny shook Duncan's shoulder, but as she did, he leapt out of bed and reached for his dirk. He flung open the door as Jenny clutched the bed clothing to her neck.

Alex ignored Duncan's state of undress and said, "There's a fire. It's your home."

With haste, Duncan pulled on his trews as he glanced back at Jenny.

Waving him on, Jenny said, "Go! I'll catch up with you." Duncan nodded and left with Alex. When Alex had gone, Jenny hurried to dress, and followed after. She rode a horse from Callum's stable and arrived to find the cottage a smoldering pile of charred planks in the midst of the stone walls.

Duncan met her as she rushed to him and asked, "Where are your parents?"

"They're fine. Only my mother was home, and some wee lads saw the fire and got help."

"What happened?"

Duncan's silence was condemning.

Jenny shook her head. "No, my father couldnae do such a thing."

"I said nothing of your father," said Duncan.

"But you thought it."

Duncan did not reply. Instead, he turned and said, "I must care for my mother."

Hastily following at his heels, Jenny said, "Is she hurt?"

He spoke over his shoulder. "She breathed in some smoke." Duncan arrived at his mother's side. She was well tended by friends. Duncan knelt. With disgust, he spoke quietly to her. "Were you alone?"

His mother gave him a calm, but knowing, look. "I'm fine, lad. Dinnae fash yersel."

Duncan clenched his jaw, but said nothing.

Nellie, said, "We're lucky to have seen it in time to keep it from spreading."

"Who saw it?" asked Duncan.

"The young lads were playing and saw a man ride by with a torch, so they ran to fetch help."

"Tavish."

"It could be, but he wore a cloth over his face, so we cannae be certain."

With a pointed look, Duncan said, "Who do you think it was?"

Without hesitation, she said, "I've nae doubt it was Tavish."

Duncan said, "I've nae doubt I will kill him the next time I see him."

Jenny touched Duncan's shoulder.

Alex opened his mouth to speak, but stopped as he heard someone singing.

With mounting anger, Duncan turned toward the approaching sound.

Alex held out his palm. "I'll take care of it."

"You mean you'll protect him," said Duncan. "For if he comes within my reach, I'll put my hands about his sorry drunk neck."

Duncan's mother reached a gentle hand out to him. "No, love. You willnae." She wheezed and coughed.

"And why shouldn't I? Ma, he left you to burn."

"No, laddie. He left me to drink. He didnae know this would happen."

Duncan muttered. "Does he know that I hate him?"

"Don't talk so."

"I'm sorry, Ma, but–"

"There is naught to be done, except fetch me some water."

Duncan rose to find water, but Nellie stopped him. "I've water right here." As Elspeth sipped from the cup of water, Duncan's father arrived. Through eyes bright with drink, he looked at his wife. "Are you hurt, darlin'?" Brodie pulled her into his arms. "I'm sorry. I should have been here."

Duncan got up and walked a way. He cast one

glance down at his mother in his father's arms. His jaw tightened as he bit back harsh words. The smell of charred thatch and wood clung to him as he walked away down the lane. Strong hands gripped Jenny's shoulders to keep her from following. Charlie said, "He'll not be fit company for a while."

"I know. But I hate to see him so."

Callum arrived with a horse and a cart. He went over to Duncan's parents and spoke in quiet tones of the croft by the sea.

Jenny said, "It's so easy for him."

"What is?" asked Charlie.

"He takes everything in stride, and he does what is right with such ease."

Charlie shrugged. "Och, 'tis easy to do the right thing when you're the chief's son with land and wealth at your disposal."

"It was not always like that for him, and you know it."

Nodding, Charlie said, "Since his father has acknowledged him as his son, Callum has shown himself worthy."

Jenny watched Callum crouch down beside Duncan's parents, placating their worries, while Mari tended to their comfort.

"I should help." Jenny started toward them, but Charlie held her back.

"They have help. There is no need to swarm about them."

She looked toward the path Duncan had taken, and then back to his parents. "It seems that I'm no use to anyone."

"Come with me." Charlie held out his hand.

With a smile, Jenny took it and followed him as he ambled down the narrow footpath.

"You've had quite a night."

Jenny glanced at him and blushed. She knew Charlie too well.

With mischief in his eyes, Charlie said, "That's not quite to what I was referring, but since you've brought up the subject, you've had quite a night, have you?"

"Charlie!" She pushed him away and kept walking. "You're a terrible man!"

"I try my best."

Jenny said, "*Och!* I dinnae know why I bother with you at all."

"Because we've been friends our whole lives and you haven't a choice anymore."

"Aye, well that much is true." She hooked her arm into his. "And as much as I hate to admit it, I'm lucky to have you."

"That's what all the lassies say," Charlie said with a satisfied grin.

They walked along for a time, until Jenny broke the comfortable silence with a troubled sigh. "Duncan feels every wrong deeply."

"That is how Duncan always has been. You cannae change a man's nature."

"I dinnae want to. I just want to help him, but there's nothing to do."

"You married him. You make him happy."

Jenny gave a wry laugh. "Happy? Without me, he'd have a home and his parents would be asleep in their bed now."

"You cannae help what others do."

"I suppose you are right."

Charlie stopped and took hold of her shoulders as he peered at her. "Dearie, I am always right."

She laughed, in spite of herself, and was met with one of Charlie's most charming grins.

He nodded toward a tree by the lake, where Duncan often went to think through his troubles. There he sat facing the water.

With a grateful smile, she said, "Charlie, you're not so terrible, really."

"Wheesht! I'll not have such talk." Charlie shooed her away and watched until she was safely at Duncan's side.

Jenny sat beside Duncan and watched the rising sun cast a path over the water to burn off the mist that still clung to the trees.

Duncan put his hand over hers.

She said, "Dinnae leave me like that again."

"It has naught to do with you."

"It has now, for you've made me your wife."

He searched her eyes with a puzzled expression.

Jenny was quiet but firm. "If you carry a burden, I'll share it."

"Jenny." He shook his head as he turned.

"Duncan," she answered right back. "If you love me, then look at me now."

He turned and faced her out of spite, but with tears in his eyes. She had never seen him like this, and her heart broke to see it. She rose to her knees so she could circle her arms about his neck. There she held him. The broken coin hung from her neck. Duncan touched it and the skin it lay against. He reached into his sporran and brought out the other half of the coin and fitted them together.

Jenny whispered, "I am yours, but you are mine, too. I'll not have you hurting alone."

A gentle rain fell in light drops on the leaves. A cool breeze sent whispers through the trees. Underneath, the two sheltered and made love. They were tender and close, with nothing between them but trust.

Chapter 11

A Croft by the Sea

THEY ARRIVED AT THE CROFT BY THE SEA. DUNCAN, Jenny and his parents settled into the croft, while the men and an insistent Mari made camp near the site where the new croft would be. Callum quickly found it was useless to argue for her comfort. She would sleep with her husband out under the stars rather than take shelter inside without him.

Brodie changed after the fire. Duncan refused to believe it would last, but Jenny did not agree. Brodie took more care with Elspeth to make her life easier. Perhaps the fire made him see he would lose her someday, and he now was reluctant to leave her alone. He drank less, and worked more to prepare for the winter. He found a good spot for the still, and made plans for the spring. They could make enough whisky to pay for their rent and sell what was left for provisions. Even in winter they could gather seaweed that the waves washed to the shore, and then burn it to make kelp. What they couldn't use themselves, they could sell. It would be a harsh first winter with no harvest or goods stored to prepare them, but before they left, Duncan's friends promised to be back with supplies to see them through the winter. After that, they would have what they needed to build a life here. At last, Duncan looked forward to the future.

The bitter sea wind drove them inside the small croft much of the time. There were two box beds arranged head to toe, with linen mattresses stuffed with hay. Despite the walls that surrounded the box beds, they were so close together that they could not help but hear any movement or whisper. While Jenny quietly coped, Duncan was sure he would go mad. In the daylight, he behaved like a thief in the mercat, touching her hand or the small of her back when he thought no one would see. The mere return of a glance made him ache to take her on the spot.

One day, the sun shone and the wind calmed. Duncan watched Jenny bend over and slide bannock dough from a spade to the bannock stone. "Ma, can you tend to that? 'Tis time I teach Jenny how to fish."

Jenny's brow wrinkled. "I've fished in the loch since I was a wee one."

Duncan nodded amiably. "But sea fishing is different." He followed that with a deep glare, which Jenny seemed slow to catch onto.

Brodie sat at the table and observed with only a glint in his eye to betray his amusement.

Elspeth said, "Away with you both. 'Tis a clear day. A walk in the fresh air will do you both good."

Brodie was quick to agree. "Aye, fresh air and a brisk walk."

Jenny wiped her hands on her apron before taking it off to hang up. "Alright, then." With a suspicious frown, Jenny put on a thick sweater and wrapped her arisaid about her. She gave a quick glance back in annoyance as Duncan pressed his hand to the small of her back to rush her through the doorway and closed it behind him.

"Lass, are your wits thick as porridge?"

"No more than yours. You've gone daft."

"No, I know very well what I'm doing." With that, concealed by the hanging folds of her arisaid, he slipped his arm about her waist just a little too high, and cupped her full breast in his hand.

With wide eyes, Jenny pushed his wrist down. "Your parents will see!"

Duncan tightened his strong arm and pulled her against him. Jenny's eyes widened more at his wicked expression. "Well, wife, you'd best hurry along before I give them something to look at." With a laugh, Duncan grabbed her wrist and pulled her along down the path.

Some distance down the shoreline, Duncan led Jenny to a small cave he had found on one of his fishing outings. He lit a fire and spread out an old plaid he had left there. As Jenny warmed her hands over the fire, Duncan touched her shoulders and touched his lips to her ear. "I've gone mad with want of you." He slid his hands down her arms and then held his hands out to warm them over the fire as he kissed the satin smooth skin of her neck. When his hands were warm, he slid them up under her sweater and pulled it up over her head.

"Duncan, it's cold!"

"I will warm you," he assured her, as he untied her shift and explored every curve his hands found. "Do you know how I suffer to watch you, unable to touch you?"

With a sharp breath, Jenny turned and kissed him.

"Are you feeling warmer yet?" he said with a gleam in his eyes.

"Aye," she sighed as she slipped her hand inside the waist of his trews.

At last unrestrained, they pulled off each other's clothing and took what they wanted with unstifled gasps and moans.

Afterward they lay wrapped together in plaids by the fire. Duncan stroked Jenny's hair as he said, "My sweet, darlin' Jenny, I'm afraid that we have a wee problem."

"There are no problems today," she said, smiling.

"I'm sorry, but there is one."

Jenny sighed. "What?"

"We will need to return with some fish, else they might wonder what we've been doing for all for this time."

"They'll think we couldnae catch any."

"I suppose that might solve that problem."

"So now there's another problem?"

With a pitiable nod, Duncan said, "I've a hunger."

Jenny lifted her eyes with some disbelief.

"For food," Duncan added with a grin. "Although, now you tempt me."

Jenny lifted her chin and smiled sweetly. "My braw

man, if we stay here much longer, they'll know well what we've been doing."

"And what of it?" He wrapped his arms around her and nuzzled his face in her neck. "Can a man not love his wife?"

Jenny could not help but smile—until his lips reached her ear. She took a halting breath in. "You'd best stop that, or we'll be bringing fish home for breakfast." She reached over and grabbed the fishing poles and handed them to Duncan while she picked up the creel. "Now go douse the fire so we can be on our way."

Duncan shook his head and did as he was told. "You're a bossy wife, aren't you?" Duncan put his arm around Jenny's shoulder. "But I've married you, so there's no hope for me now."

"*Och*, you poor lad!" Jenny gave him a playful shove and ran on without him.

MOST NIGHTS, they sat close to the fire. After Duncan and Brodie had finished carving trenchers and forks to eat with, they spent weeks making a chess board and pieces. The two men often played chess while the women knitted wool sweaters and socks. This evening, Jenny caught Elspeth watching Brodie with a slight smile. Since coming here, he had stopped drinking. Duncan had already sold most of the whisky by the time their cottage burned down. The few bottles left had gone untouched. As they played chess, Duncan and Brodie talked easily. Duncan showed a respect for his father that Jenny had not seen before. They were a family again, and now she was part of it. She returned to her knitting, content.

Duncan was not. As winter drew out, the gray weather wore on his spirit. More than once, Jenny saw him stare out at the water, and she knew he was restless. He had spent time at sea, and she feared that he missed it. She had always assumed that his restless spirit was caused by his troubles with Brodie. She saw now it was not. His parents were settled and happy, with a means of supporting themselves. Come the spring, she would not be surprised if he wanted to leave their new home, but she would not be happy about it. No matter what he decided, she had made her own decision. She would be by his side.

Spring crept in with a lingering chill, but the air smelled of new life. Duncan hitched his horse to the cart. They needed provisions. They were nearly out of food, and soon they would need seed for planting.

Jenny trailed behind him as he made preparations, clutching her arisaid about her. "You cannae go without me."

"I've made up my mind, and I'll not argue with you."

"Well I've made up my mind, and I will! You'll not leave me here alone!"

"You'll not be alone. My parents are here."

"And I love them, but I want to be with you."

"What happened to the timid girl I married?"

"I've learned to be strong."

Duncan gave her an admiring gaze. "So you have, and I'm proud of you for it."

Jenny leaned close so her lips nearly touched his. "Then take me with you."

Duncan shook his head and gently held her at bay.

"I want to go." She was quiet but firm.

No." He turned and exhaled.

"*Och*, dinnae heave sighs at me."

"Will you tell me how to breathe now, woman?"

"I will. And you'll not breathe at all unless I am with you. And if I go with you, I may let you breathe heavily." Jenny smiled.

Duncan could not help but grin as he turned and pulled her into his embrace. "Jenny, darlin'." He kissed the frown on her forehead. "I would like nothing more than to have you at my side, but we dinnae know what state of mind your father is in, let alone Tavish."

"It's been months. Do you really think they're still angry?"

"Clans have fought for generations over less."

"But I'm not a laird's daughter. I'm not worth a clan war."

"You are to me. I would fight for you, but I'd rather not do it today."

Jenny did not try to hide her disappointment. She would not give up. "Let me talk to my father."

Duncan shook his head resolutely.

Jenny said, "If you let a wound fester, it only gets worse. If we go home together, we can make amends with my father and perhaps even Tavish."

Duncan could not deny that it might make things

better, but it could make matters worse. Still, he considered it.

Having gained ground, Jenny went on. "He'll forgive us when he sees how happy I am with you."

"Perhaps he will, but Tavish willnae. I'll not put you in danger."

With frank disbelief, Jenny said, "Tavish wouldnae hurt me, and he cannae hurt you. You're much stronger than he is."

Duncan looked squarely at her. "Do you think you can flatter me into letting you have your way?"

"I was hoping."

Duncan laughed and gazed up at the sky. "God help me." To Jenny, he hastened to say, "I'm not fool enough to be swayed by your flirtatious ways."

Jenny shook her head and whispered, "No, you are far too strong-minded for that." She had won, and she knew it. A smile bloomed on her face.

Duncan shook his head, but a faint smile betrayed him. "I'll let you come because what you said makes some sense."

"Of course it does. Now, about your breathing." She leaned close and hooked her hands over the waist of his trews. I thought we might stop on the way."

Duncan raised an eyebrow. "Have you planned the journey for me, too?"

"No, just one part of it." She gave him a quick peck on the cheek. "I'll go pack now."

"Hurry," Duncan called after, with a mischievous glint in his eye.

THEY ARRIVED at Callum's house, after passing the burned shell of Duncan's old cottage. Duncan was in no mood to discuss Jenny's family, which was all she could think of. She had not left them in the way that she should, and she felt badly for it. All she wanted was to rush home and throw her arms about her mother and tell her she was sorry for the trouble she had caused. Her father would be displeased with her, but he would forgive her. She felt certain of it.

They reached Callum and Mari's house as the dusk settled about them. Mari fed them a hearty meal and asked all about how they had fared for the winter. The large fireplace warmed away the chill of the early spring night.

At last, Jenny said, "Tell me more of my parents. You've said very little about them." They had talked about nearly everyone else, until it was clear there was something amiss.

Callum looked at her directly, and did not mince words. "There is trouble."

Jenny braced herself.

"They are well enough." Callum reached out and put his hand on Jenny's to calm her. "It's to do with money. I know only because I have been helping my father to manage the estate. Between a laird and his tacksman, there are certain financial dealings. Funds have gone missing that were under your father's care."

Jenny said, "I am sure he will right any wrong that has happened on his watch."

Callum smiled sympathetically. "Money doesnae go missing like that unless someone is doing something they shouldnae be doing."

"Are you saying my father stole from your father?"

"I'm sorry, Jenny. I only know that money is missing. If there's a proper reason, your father has yet to offer it."

"You make him sound like a common thief."

"That was not my intention. I meant only to prepare you. Unless your father can restore the missing money, he will no longer be tacksman."

"But our home…"

Callum delivered the news as gently as anyone could. "You must know that he lives there at the pleasure of the laird. As it is, I have convinced my father to show mercy, as it is his first offense."

Duncan went to Jenny and stood behind her chair with his hands on her shoulders. No one spoke of it, but they all knew that thieves could be punished by having an ear or a hand cut off, by being branded on the cheek and banished, or even by hanging.

Callum said, "But there is still a matter of the missing funds, I'm afraid. If they are not restored, your parents will be banished."

Too shocked to absorb what she was hearing, Jenny said, "My father a criminal? My mother must be distraught. I must go to them."

Duncan said, "We will go in the morning."

Bereft, Jenny tried to absorb it.

Duncan thanked Mari and Callum for their hospitality, and urged Mari not to trouble herself. They would find their own way to the same room where they had spent their wedding night.

How different tonight was. Jenny was already weary from traveling here. This news had shaken her too much to express it. She simply readied herself for bed and curled up close to Duncan.

Duncan held her in his arms. "Your father is a very smart man. He will see his way through this and take care of your mother. And I will always take care of you. You need not worry yourself."

But she did, for the life she had known was unhinged. She said softly, "What will they do? I cannae imagine them poor, having to live in a croft somewhere."

Duncan took her words like a sharp blow. She was too weary to think of how she had sounded to Duncan. She drifted asleep to escape from her worries, but Duncan did not. He lay awake thinking of how he had dragged her down to a lowly life in a croft. She had been raised for a much different life. He had taken for granted that she would adjust and be happy, for they were in love. Now he wondered if love would always be enough.

THE MACRUER HOUSE was a good walk away from Callum's house. Callum had offered one of his horses so the two could reach Jenny's parents sooner. Jenny silently rode. Duncan took note, and assumed the weight of her silence as his own. He could not forget what she had said before falling asleep. It put distance between them, which he had never felt before. She was higher born. He had always known it. But growing up as they had, the wall between them had been long ago breached. There had only been love between them. So, when she spoke of her parents not having to stoop to his level, the words cut him.

They now rode along the same paths they had ridden before. The landscape was the same, but so much had happened that could not be undone. They had changed. It was no longer the home they once knew.

DUNCAN GAVE Jenny's hand a squeeze as they stood at the door to her house.

Her mother answered the door and threw her arms about Jenny. She gave Duncan a warm nod, but no more. As she invited them inside, she said, "I'm sorry. The servants have been given the day off."

Jenny took a seat beside Duncan. "The day off, Mum? Tell me the truth."

Rowena MacRuer's expression crumbled as she shook her head.

Jenny said, "What happened?"

"You should hear that from your father. I know very little. He willnae talk to me about it."

"Will he see us?" asked Jenny.

"I dinnae know, lass. He was so angry with you when you left."

"I'm sorry." Jenny wanted to say more. There was no denying the pain she had caused, even though they had left her no other choice.

Jenny's mother reached out and clasped Jenny's hands. "Are you happy?"

"I am. But I'm worried about you."

"You've a life of your own. You need not worry about us."

"You're my parents. Of course I will worry."

Rowena smoothed her hair back from her face. "I'm certain your father will sort it all out."

Jenny nodded, as if agreeing, although she could not be so sure. "May I see him?"

"He's not himself."

"Please. I must see him."

Her mother was hesitant, but led them to the study. Andrew, with hair in disarray, looked up from his desk and closed the drawer gently. His blank look did not reveal any emotion toward her, but his sharp glance at Duncan left no doubt how he felt toward him.

Duncan was first to speak. "Mr. MacRuer, I beg your forgiveness for the pain I have caused you and your family."

Andrew regarded him quizzically, but said nothing.

Duncan went on, "I love your daughter, and would give my life to see her safe and happy."

"You might better have done that before you stole her from us and a life that was worthy of her."

Duncan took his sharp words without flinching. Only a dark look in his eyes betrayed his reaction. "She wanted to go."

"She didnae know what she was doing."

Duncan took a moment to tamp down words he would regret. Instead, he said, "We had promised ourselves to each other."

"What did you promise her? A croft with walls blackened by soot, where she'd spend bitter winters huddled by the fire for warmth? Did you promise her hands rough and callused?"

Jenny hid her hands in the folds of her skirts.

Duncan said, "I know it was not what you'd hoped for your daughter. I can promise you that she is dearly loved."

Andrew scoffed.

Jenny leaned forward. "Father! Dinnae laugh so at my husband!"

Andrew was visibly taken aback. He stared at her, first with shock, then with scorn. "Listen to you, bold as brass. Why, you're ready for life as a merchant's wife, hawking your wares in the mercat."

Duncan took in a sharp breath, but Jenny spoke before he could. "I would be proud to do it, for there is no better life than to stand beside the man I love and to know he loves me. Duncan's love is far dearer to me than all of your money." She stopped short.

Andrew had no retort, for he had no money. In that moment, they all knew that any station Andrew had held had been lost. He was no higher than Duncan, and he knew it. Jenny had not intended to do so, but her words had brought him down to a place he did not want to be. Thus bitterly humbled, words failed him.

Andrew was no longer the commanding father to whom Jenny had always looked up. He was powerless now, and she felt pity for him. Jenny sank into a chair and leaned her hands on the desk. "Father, what happened?"

Duncan stood stiffly by her side.

Andrew poured himself a drink and offered one to

Duncan. "Years ago, my friends and I formed a tontine. We pooled our money and shared the dividends every year. I was charged with keeping the account and disbursing the money. I was once short of money, years ago. So I borrowed from the principal. No one knew, and I paid it all back from the rents I collected. It was always temporary."

"Always? So you did it again?"

"Many times. No one was hurt. I paid it back. That is, until a few years ago. I was short. But I always made the dividend payments, so no one found out."

"Some months ago, before the lads all went to the lowlands to fight, I was late with the dividend payment. Malcolm MacLean demanded to see the ledger."

"Tavish's father?"

"He and I were the last members of the tontine."

Duncan put a hand on Jenny's shoulder as he guessed what was coming.

"He knew what I'd done. I owed him far more than I could ever repay." Andrew's eyes rested on Jenny. "Tavish fancied you. Quite a lot."

"Enough to accept her as payment?" Andrew looked down and nodded.

"Father, you sold me?"

Andrew looked at her. "We made a marriage arrangement. Such things are done all the time."

"Not to satisfy a debt. Men do not barter their daughters."

With sorrow, Andrew said, "But they do."

"Jenny, dear, it was a very good match," said her mother.

Her words were of no use. For all of her life, Jenny had trusted her father. But he was a thief, and she was no more than a business commodity. Jenny leaned back in her chair and studied her rough, callused hands. She said softly, "I would rather sell whisky at mercat than to be sold."

"Jenny, please understand."

"Do you think Tavish would have loved me knowing that he'd won me like a prize?"

"He did know."

Jenny nodded. "And he held no affection, nor any respect for me."

"It angered him greatly to lose you," said Andrew.

"Because of his pride," Jenny hastened to say. "But he never loved me."

"After you left, he went into a rage. He demanded compensation. But with no money left in the tontine, he settled for revenge. He went to the Laird of Glengarry. I'm sure it was his plan to repay his public humiliation with mine. But Glengarry has been good enough to keep it private."

Jenny reached for Duncan's hand.

Andrew gazed at his wife. "I am sorry, good wife."

Rowena's sympathy shone through her distress.

Before she could speak, Andrew opened his desk drawer and pulled out a pistol. Pushing Jenny behind him, Duncan lunged over the desk and grabbed hold of Andrew's forearm to keep him from pointing it at himself. A hissing sound and a puff of smoke rose from the pistol, and then nothing. Duncan forced the pistol from Andrew's hand as Rowena rushed to her husband's side. "Are you hurt?"

Andrew stared at his desk without expression. "No, much to my misfortune."

Duncan said, "You're lucky the main charge failed to ignite. Give me your word that you'll not try that again."

Andrew did not respond right away, but a tear trailed down his face. His voice broke as he said, "You have my word." He fell into his wife's arms and wept.

Jenny stared at her father. She had never seen him cry, or express any emotion like this.

After a quick search of the desk, Duncan found what he needed to remove the ball and clean the powder from the barrel. With that done, he slid the pistol into his belt. "I'll keep this for you for now." Pulling Jenny aside, he asked, "Are there any more guns in here?"

"Not that I know of."

While Rowena tended to Andrew, Duncan led Jenny outside. As he closed the door, Jenny said, "I should do something."

"They are best left alone, for now."

With Jenny's hand still in his grasp, Duncan led her on a walk to nowhere in particular, just away from the house. "You'll not blame yourself."

"I dinnae know what you mean."

"Yes, you do. You may lie to yourself, but do not lie to me."

Jenny walked on in silence.

"This was not your fault." He lifted her chin and searched her eyes. "Nor was it mine."

Jenny lifted rueful eyes. "And yet, here we are at the center of it."

Duncan stopped and pulled her into his arms. "I'll hear no more talk like that. We may have been at the center, but we were not the cause. Your own father admitted it."

"That's little comfort when your parents and now mine have had their lives torn apart. All the people we love have been hurt."

A fierce look burned in Duncan's eyes. "Tavish MacLean has had his revenge."

Chapter 12

The Harvest

DUNCAN HELPED ANDREW STOW THE TRUNKS ON THE carriage Rowena's sister and husband had sent for them. Her sister had married a wealthy merchant. Andrew had always looked down upon him for being in trade, but now the merchant would be able to look down upon them. They had become the poor relations, and Rowena's sister and husband were taking them in. They would live in his grand house in Glasgow until Andrew could put their lives back together.

"Must you leave right away?" Jenny asked them.

Rowena touched her palm to Jenny's cheek. "We must put this life behind us. It will be better for your father." Tears welled in her eyes.

Andrew was not himself. Nor would he be, Jenny feared. She promised to visit as she held her mother close and bade her goodbye. She gave her father a kiss on the cheek. He could barely bring his red-rimmed

eyes to meet hers. When he did, all she saw there was
sadness.

Duncan offered his hand as Rowena stepped into
the carriage. She was grateful, and showed it. He had
saved her husband's life. There were no words for that,
nor did Duncan expect them. The carriage drove off,
but the unbidden weight of their sorrow remained.

Duncan and Jenny stayed with Callum and Mari for a
time. They had a large house, which they were glad to
share. Summer came, and its warmth and long days
had a healing effect upon Jenny. In the mornings,
Callum and Duncan practiced swordplay at the castle
with Alex, Charlie and their clansmen. There were
rumors of being called back into service, but none
came to fruition. In the afternoons, Duncan and Jenny
helped Callum with chores. While their house was
grand, their income was not. There was always work to
do, and Duncan and Jenny were glad for the chance to
help out. Night fell late in the summer, so they had long
evenings to walk and dream together of the future. Life
was as they once hoped it would be after marriage,
with days of contentment, and nights of passion.

The time came to deliver more food and supplies
to Duncan's parents. They were producing enough
kelp to pay for most of it. Soon the first barley crop
would be harvested and they would begin to make
whisky.

On a cool summer evening, joined by Alex and

Charlie, they all sat by the fire talking and laughing. When the conversation fell into a comfortable lull, Callum said, "We've not had enough evenings like this."

Mari said, "Aye, it's true. This reminds me of our days together in Edinburgh."

While they had shared many fine evenings together, they had shared tragedy, too. Duncan eyed them skeptically. "We have been here since spring. Are you not tired of us yet?"

Mari smiled. "Never." "We have not seen Alex and Charlie as much as we'd like." Mari look to them both for agreement.

Duncan glanced at the men with a smirk. "That lot is but minutes away, and we've trained together every day."

Mari met Alex's eyes with a knowing expression.

Taking her cue, Alex said, "*Och*, Duncan. In truth, do you not wish for those days?"

"No," Duncan said bluntly. "I do not."

Alex chuckled. "Of course you do. Don't we all?"

When no answer came forth, Alex gave Charlie a sharp elbow to the ribs.

"Aye! More time together!" Charlie said as though waking up.

Duncan glanced at Jenny. They both turned toward the others, whose eyes twinkled mischievously.

Silence stretched awkwardly on until Mari said, "The truth is, we thought it a nice time to go spend by the sea. We were all hoping there might be some barley to harvest, and a croft to build."

Jenny grinned. "'Tis a fine idea! Would you really do that for us?"

"Not for Duncan," said Callum with a wink. But for you and his parents we will." He leaned forward. "However, there is one condition." He turned to Duncan, in earnest, but made him wait for the rest. "I would have a dram or two of your whiskey."

With a broad smile, Duncan said, "It will be yours. But if it doesnae taste good, blame the harvest workers."

"I will do just that."

Duncan leaned back, content to have such good friends.

A DRIVING rain welcomed them back to the croft on the coast.

"'Tis a good thing that I thought to bring a tent." The corner of Callum's mouth quirked up as he caught Mari's eye. They both knew that she had reminded him of it.

Duncan pointed out a suitable place to pitch the tent, and they set to work. The rain had blown over by morning, but they waited another day for the barley to dry enough to harvest. Duncan thought they should wait one more day, but Brodie disagreed. The best chance for a few days of sunshine was right after a rain. So they went to the fields when the dew had burned off and the sun was high in the sky. A strong sea breeze braced their spirits as they faced the task before them.

The men cut their way down long rows with sickles, while the women followed to gather and bundle the grain. Jenny stole more than a few glances at Duncan as he bent over to work. His shirt, damp from sweat, clung to his broad shoulders and muscular arms. Her eyes traced a path from his torso to his backside and powerful thighs. Hard work had its rewards, she decided. Her thoughts thus focused, she did not hear Charlie approach. Nor did she see him follow her gaze and grin as he guessed her thoughts. Charlie cleared his throat loudly.

"*Och*, Charlie, you startled me!" Jenny pressed her hand to her chest.

"So I see. You seemed deep in thought." If his knowing weren't enough, he glanced back at Duncan and then at her, grinning.

Unable to deflect Charlie's unabashed teasing, Jenny blushed and turned away.

Charlie chuckled. The others all stopped working and headed for the barrel of water. Charlie poured a dipper of water over his head.

Duncan sat down beside Jenny, and joined her in leaning against a stack of bundles. "I'm sorry that you have to do field work."

Charlie overheard and offered, with a wink, "She has a fine eye for this sort of work, haven't you, Jenny?"

Duncan seemed confused. "I dinnae know that it takes as much eye as it does muscle."

Charlie nodded, "Aye, well, your Jenny appreciates both, don't you Jenny?"

Jenny picked up a handful of stray stalks and threw

them at Charlie, who was already ducking. "Away with you!"

Charlie brushed the barley from his hair and clothing as he rose to go after more water.

Jenny blushed as she explained to Duncan, "Charlie caught me admiring you as you worked. You're very braw."

Duncan's eyes smoldered with unexpressed thoughts. "You're a fine worker, yourself, lass." He glanced down at the moist neckline of her shift and blew gently on her chest to cool her. His lips spread into a slight smile as she leaned her head back against the barley stack. With a sigh, she closed her eyes.

Duncan said, "Your arms and back will be sore from the work." He proceeded to rub her shoulders and neck.

Callum announced that he was going back to work, and everyone followed. Duncan and Jenny exchanged a wistful look, and then joined the others.

At the end of the day, they went down to the shore.

Charlie announced, "Take heed, lassies! I'll not swim in my plaid, so turn your heads or not. Tis your choice." By the time he had said it, his plaid lay in a heap on the rocks, and his leine was next to follow.

With a gasp, Mari turned. "Charlie, you gave us no time!"

Jenny laughed and called out. "He's a proud man, Mari. We're still not sure why." Mari was too shocked to laugh, but the men chuckled and called out their agreement.

The other men showed no shame in unwrapping their plaids and running into the water, as they had done many times in the loch since they were young children. But Mari, steeped in her lowland Covenanter upbringing, was unused to their wild Highland ways. For her sake, Jenny discreetly alerted her when the men were fully immersed in the water. For years, Jenny had felt like one of the lads. There was nothing any of them could do anymore that she could not dismiss with a roll of her eyes. She should have minded their antics, but she did not.

Jenny said, "This may shock you, but I'm going in there, too."

Mari was not shocked, but neither was she ready to take off all but her shift to go into the water with a group of naked men, even if her husband was one of them. "You go on, Jenny. I'll wade in to my ankles."

Callum called out to Mari, "Wear your shift into the water. We'll all turn around until you're all the way in."

Charlie said, "I'll make no such promises, dearie!"

Callum practically growled. "Lad, you can look away on your own, or I'll have you looking away under water."

Charlie laughed. "You're not as much fun as you used to be!"

Mari said, "Oh, but Charlie, he is!"

It was Charlie's turn to be caught off guard. For once, he was at a loss for words.

Meanwhile, Callum came out of the water such as he was, and scooped the fully clothed Mari into his arms, and carried her over his shoulder and into the water. Jenny laughed as she removed all but her shift and ran after. Duncan waved and swam toward her, meeting her in shoulder-deep water. He planted a kiss that took her breath away, as his hands explored all they could find under the water.

"Duncan! The others." She warned him.

"They cannae see me do this."

Jenny gasped.

"Or this."

"Oh!" Her eyes were quite round. Duncan's smile dissolved and a dark expression took its place. "I've been yearning for you." His warm breath brushed her ear.

"Well, you'll not have me here!" She whispered, frantically.

He held her against him so his lips brushed hers as he spoke. "Tonight. We'll sneak out under moonlight. I want to hear you sigh my name as we lie on a bed of fresh-cut barley."

Jenny glanced about to make sure no one saw the exquisite torment he could cause under water.

"Tonight, then?"

"Aye." It came out as a sigh. "Now, please stop." With reluctance, she gently pushed him away.

He took her face in his hands and touched his forehead to hers. "Know this, Jenny, my love. Between now and then, every time I look at you, I'll be thinking of us in the barley, and what I will do to coax another sigh from you."

She looked away to be sure no one was watching, sure that her thoughts could be read on her face. "And I will have thoughts of my own."

No one was watching because everyone else was on their way out of the water. Some stood on the shore. Jenny asked, and Duncan saw to it, that the men turn away as she emerged with her linen shift clinging to her body. She hid behind jutting rocks as she squeezed out the water until the shift hung loosely. Then she gathered up her clothes and walked back to the croft while her shift dried. Duncan slipped his hand into hers, and they lingered behind the others. Jenny hoped she would never lose the thrill his touch brought her.

He smiled down at her, and lifted a brow as his gaze swept over her breasts. "You should put on your bodice."

"But my shift is still damp."

"Aye, it is that." Duncan hooked his arm about her neck and drew her close to his side while he whispered into her ear. "And, while it is a bonnie sight, I would rather it be only mine to see."

Jenny followed his gaze to her chest. Her wet linen shift was translucent and clung to her curves. Mortified, she glanced up at his smoldering eyes.

Without a word, Jenny hastily pulled on her bodice and skirts as she worked to keep pace with the others.

Duncan stopped along the way and drew her into his arms. Making sure that his back concealed it, he smoothed his hand down the center of her bodice. "Do you have it still?"

With a soft smile, Jenny said, "I do." She slid the busk from its center channel between rows of stays in her bodice.

Duncan ran his thumb over the crudely carved whalebone scrimshaw he had made while at sea. "I had lost you, but my heart wouldnae let go." Whatever he had meant to say after that was lost to unutterable emotion.

Jenny put her hand over his hand, still grasping the busk, and she whispered the words carved in it. "My heart can be nowhere else." She slipped it back into its place.

LATE INTO THE NIGHT, Jenny tiptoed across the cottage floor, flinching as Brodie let out a shuddering snore. Duncan stifled a laugh as he steadied Jenny and led her outside. With the door closed behind them, they snickered and ran away as if they were children. The full moon lit their way. Duncan scooped Jenny up by the waist and spun her about. Then he kissed her.

They made their way kissing and stumbling to a stack of barley, where Duncan wasted no time pulling off Jenny's shift. As he did so, she pulled his leine up until her skin met his.

Duncan said softly, "I have wanted to taste you since you walked out of the water. All of you." With hands and mouth he touched her and teased her until she was panting and clutching at him. Jenny wrapped her legs around him and reveled in the physical power of his need for her. She needed him, too, as much then as after, when they lay suspended in bliss. Later, long after they lay on their backs watching the stars, they would need the fullness and the trust of that moment. It bound them together.

Chapter 13

Unspoken Promises

ELSPETH SET DOWN A LOAF OF BARLEY BREAD MADE from the first grains of the harvest. Beside it were smoked salmon, kale and baked apples. The men offered hearty approval as Brodie brought in one of the last bottles of the whisky he had brought from home. Lively talk went back and forth across the table, and laughter filled the croft. Duncan grinned and muttered something that made Charlie laugh. Jenny looked at her family and friends, and she thought of how good her life was.

Brodie said, "With the harvest done, we can start on your croft, lad."

Duncan nodded appreciatively.

"We've enough hands here to have it done in a sennight," said Alex.

Charlie shook his head slightly. "*Och*, less than that."

"Perhaps." Alex turned to Callum for his opinion, but instead paused to study him. "What is it?"

Callum exhaled. "I dinnae want to talk about this until after the harvest."

"Well, the harvest is over, so tell us." Alex could see this would not be good news.

Callum smiled with false cheer. "It's too fine an evening. Let us talk in the morning."

The room was still. No one spoke. Mari watched her husband, while the others shared questioning glances.

Finally, Duncan spoke up. "There's no use, Callum. We know that there's something on your mind. Until you tell us, we'll think of nothing else."

"Aye," said Callum. "There is something, but I dinnae like it." He studied his hands for a moment. "As chief, my father has a duty to the king."

"To raise troops." Alex said bluntly.

Elspeth let out a small moan. Brodie put a comforting hand on hers.

"What has happened?" Jenny asked. "I thought you put down the Covenanter rebellion."

"Not enough, so it seems." Callum shared a look with Mari, and then looked frankly at Jenny. "The king has asked the Glengarry to raise troops. I will go. Will you go with me?"

"Not Duncan." Jenny turned to him. "Duncan, you dinnae have to go."

Duncan met her gaze with eyes full of his own inner struggle.

"I almost lost you once. How can I let you go now?" Jenny could not contain her emotions. She rose quickly and went outside.

Duncan watched her and then turned to Callum. "I will go."

Callum nodded his thanks.

Duncan excused himself to go out to Jenny. He did not see her at first.

"I'll not leave your side, Duncan," she vowed. She was leaning against the trunk of a tree, staring out at the sea. Waves of water rushed toward the land with insistent rhythm.

Duncan went to her side. "I must go, darlin'."

Jenny's self-control crumbled. "I know." She turned and threw her arms about his neck, and she pressed her body against his.

Duncan wrapped his arms tightly about her and cradled her head against him.

"I'm sorry," she said, as she cried.

"No, love. You've nothing to be sorry for."

Jenny ran her hands over his shoulders and chest. "You're mine. Why must they take you from me?"

He had no answer. Duncan held her until she stopped crying and wiped the tears from her face.

They went back inside. Elspeth watched Jenny with sympathy.

Alex said, "When do we leave?"

Callum gave a weak smile, and said, "I wanted to make sure that the harvest was in."

"Thank you for that," Brodie told him.

Callum turned to Alex. "We must leave tomorrow."

Jenny shut her eyes and tamped down her emotions.

Callum went on. "The rest of the men will be

waiting for us at the castle. We'll assemble there, and then we're for Stranraer. The Sheriff of Galloway has been replaced by John Graham of Claverhouse."

"Bluidy Clavers?" Charlie caught a sharp look from Callum and leaned back with remorse for his outburst in front of the women.

"We're to report to John Graham of Claverhouse."

Charlie caught Alex's eye, but looked away. He had already said too much.

IT WAS FITTINGLY gloomy the following morning as they readied to ride. Jenny came out of the croft, bundle in hand, and went straight to Duncan. She lifted her chin and said boldly, "I'm riding with you."

Taken aback, Duncan took a moment to react. "Are you daft? No, you willnae."

"Mari is going."

"Mari is going to her home, and you will stay in yours," Duncan said firmly.

Jenny would not back down. "I lay awake all night thinking about it."

"Not all night," he said under his breath, as he led her away to speak in private. They had spent much of the night, clinging together as they made love in the box bed. "Now be a good girl, and gie us a goodbye kiss."

"I will do neither!"

Duncan's eyes darted over to Mari and the men, who were packed and ready to go. He spoke in an awkward hush. "Dinnae do this. The others are waiting."

Jenny held her ground boldly. "I will go where you go."

Duncan's nostrils flared as he held back his anger. The others waited, and he had to go. Duncan glared at Jenny, and the fire in her eyes. The wind lashed them both and tugged the kertch from Jenny's face, freeing her hair to blow wildly about. Without thinking, Duncan reached out and smoothed the hair back from her face. This was the Jenny he would recall in the lonely hours away. He yanked her to him, and he kissed her. She was fuming and struggled, but her lips betrayed her and opened to his. After her arms softened and her body was formed against his, Duncan whispered, "Do you know how I love you?"

He stepped away, holding her hand, and with one last look, turned and let go.

She shook her head and whispered, "Don't go."

He mounted his horse.

Jenny said, "If you go without me, I will follow on foot."

Duncan steeled himself and urged his horse on without looking back. The others offered sorrowful glances, and then turned to follow.

Bereft, Jenny turned to Duncan's parents. "I must go."

Brodie started to protest, but Elspeth silenced him with her hand on his arm.

Brodie said, "Alright. Let her have her long walk, and then I'll go bring her home."

Elspeth nodded.

Jenny swallowed back tears and started to walk. The riders disappeared over a hill. Jenny held back her shoulders and lifted her chin. They could leave her behind, but she would not stay there.

From over the hill came a horseman. "Duncan," she whispered.

Duncan brought his horse to a stop beside her. His eyes burned. "God's teeth, woman. Get on."

Jenny stepped on his foot in the stirrup as he pulled her the rest of the way onto the horse. As she wrapped her arms around his waist, she turned back. Elspeth and Brodie waved as Duncan and Jenny rode over the hill.

WHILE THE WOMEN LAGGED BEHIND, talking, Callum and Duncan spoke of the task before them.

Duncan said, "The lowlanders call him Bluidy Clavers."

"Aye, so I've heard."

"They say he's a brutal man."

Callum stared gravely ahead. "They say what will serve their cause."

Duncan said, "Do you not think it's true?"

Callum's expression was grim. "I pray to God it isnae."

Mari rode up to keep pace beside her husband. "Callum," she said sweetly enough to arouse Callum's suspicion.

He looked at her and waited.

"If Jenny is going with Duncan—"

"You will wait for me at home." It came out like an order to his soldiers. With one caustic glance, Callum thanked Duncan for bringing this on him. He turned back to Mari. "As you will recall, I had no choice but to bring you with me the last time. You suffered much for it, which grieves me to this day. But we had no choice, then. We do now, and that choice is for you to stay at home where you belong."

Mari bristled but calmed herself. "Husband, you are my home." Mari did not speak to Callum again until they stopped at midday to rest the horses.

Callum found Mari sitting on a fallen log. Prepared for battle, he sat down beside her.

"You're right, of course," Mari told him. "I would be safer at home."

Callum said, "I cannae imagine what I would do if harm came to you."

She nodded. "That would be terrible for you."

"Aye, just so."

Mari said gently, "And that is what matters most, is it not? How you feel?"

Callum looked at her sideways.

Mari said, "To wait and not know whether you've been shot or run through with a sword shouldnae bother me, as long as I am safe at home."

She had dealt a blow to his heart. Callum turned his warm gaze upon her. "I'd not have you worry about me."

"I know that. Nor would I have you worry about me."

"But, Mari, I must keep you safe."

She took hold of his hand and studied its strength

and its scars. "I'd rather live by your side than be home safe and lonely." She lifted his hand to her cheek.

Callum held close and kissed her forehead. "Mari, will it ever be easy for us?"

She looked up at him. "I didnae marry you for the easy life you offered me."

Callum had to smile.

Mari said, "I fell in love with your strength and your passion. I have always felt at home in your arms. Let me stay here, where I feel safe."

Callum circled his arms about Mari and held her. The words caught in his throat. "You are dear to me, Mari."

With a kiss, they made an unspoken promise never to part.

Chapter 14

The Superior Officer

THEY ARRIVED AT THE CASTLE IN THE MARKET TOWN OF Stranraer, where Captain Claverhouse was now headquartered. Callum went inside to report, while the rest went in search of some lodgings. A pair of local young ladies caught Charlie's eye, so he lingered behind to entertain them with his charm. There was an inn that was humble but habitable, but the rooms were all taken, but one. They might have a second room in a week, the innkeeper told them. Until then, he could bring in some linen and straw for a pallet. So they took the room, grateful for someplace to stay. Alex and Charlie would try to find quarter with the other troops.

When they returned to the castle for Callum, they found him talking to a soldier near the entrance. Callum, who was facing them, smiled, but it was forced. As they neared Callum, the Lieutenant turned to face them.

Tavish MacLean greeted them with a smug smile. "What, no salute for your superior officer?"

Duncan's arm tensed as Tavish eyed him and then settled his gaze upon Jenny. Jenny squeezed Duncan's arm and then slipped her hand away while Duncan saluted Tavish.

Tavish barely noticed. His eyes were on Jenny. He nodded. "Lady–" he grinned as he corrected himself, "Mistress… do you even have a last name?"

Jenny's lips parted to answer.

Duncan said tersely, "Mrs. MacDonell."

Tavish nodded. "Ah, yes. You look different from when we last met." His gaze trailed down her plain bodice and skirts.

"As do you." Jenny lifted her chin.

His mouth quirked up at the corner, just short of a sneer.

With a withering look that brushed past Duncan, Tavish turned his attention to Callum. "You and your men will report to me in the morning. I will give you your orders then." His flinty eyes darted to Jenny for an instant, while Callum saluted and turned away, leading the way to anywhere Tavish was not. When they'd gone a safe distance, Callum said, "I'm sorry, Duncan. I dinnae know about Tavish."

"Lieutenant MacLean, to you." Charlie said, smirking.

Alex mimicked Tavish. "What, no salute?"

Charlie leapt in front of them, leaving them with no choice but to stop. "I beg your pardon! Lieutenant, I salute you!" With that, Charlie bent over and started to pull up his plaid.

Duncan gave him a good-natured kick in the back-side. "Not in front of the ladies, you wild Highlander!"

Charlie staggered a bit but recovered his balance. "*Och*, ladies, I'm sorry." He lifted Mari's hand to his lips and then raised his eyes to meet hers. Callum growled a warning, which made Charlie smile.

He then turned to Jenny, but Duncan swatted his hand away. "She accepts your apology."

Charlie laughed. "*Och*, I'm fair thirsty. I'm away to yon tavern. Will anyone care to join me?"

THE NEXT MORNING, Charlie moaned and rolled over, spreading his arm across the warm body beside him. It was promptly thrown off.

"Away with you!" Alex said. He gave Charlie a shove.

Charlie lifted his head, realized it was Alex, and grunted as he rolled over and mumbled, "Thank God. I thought I'd got so full of drink that I'd bedded a cow."

Alex gave him a swat. "No cow would have you, you oaf."

Callum said, "You can thank these good ladies for giving you quarter."

"Good ladies, I thank you," said Charlie as he hoisted himself to his feet with a groan.

Jenny gave Charlie a tolerant smile. "You're welcome, good sir."

After some porridge and ale, the men went to report to Lieutenant MacLean.

Mari saw the worry on Jenny's face. "Duncan is strong and fine. And he has good friends beside him."

"Aye," said Jenny. Her eyes did not leave Duncan until he was out of sight.

THE MEN ARRIVED at the castle to find Tavish in the bailey, on his horse and looking impatient. Captain Claverhouse was away in England and had left Tavish in charge of the Highland Dragoons. Small parties were patrolling the area while others were to visit farms known to sympathize with the Covenanters' cause.

Tavish said, "Here's a list of the locals I want you to watch. Anyone hiding or rendering aid to known Covenanters must suffer the king's justice."

"Aye," said Callum. He displayed just enough patience, which was all that he had. He and his men had spent months on a similar mission. "You'll recall that we've done this before."

"I do. And I also recall that you married the enemy."

"Not all of them, mind, just the one," Charlie muttered under his breath, while Alex pretended not to hear.

Duncan's voice had an edge to it. "He did his duty—and more, and he nearly gave his life for the crown. Callum MacDonell is one of our finest. No man can deny it."

"I can," said Tavish.

Callum appeared calm, except for an occasional twitch of his jaw muscles. He observed Tavish as if from a distance.

Tavish said, "You're a fine soldier, Callum, but you cannae deny you were too soft on the family. You could have saved yourself a good deal of trouble. That's what comes from letting your heart rule your brain."

"I will bear that in mind." Callum's face was devoid of emotion, his posture erect.

"I'll expect more than that. I'll expect you to make an example of every Covenanter you catch."

Alex and Charlie exchanged sideways glances. Alex said, "An example?"

Tavish gave a curt nod. "The privy council has given us the authority to execute fugitives from the law."

Charlie, unusually somber, eyed Tavish with disbelief. "You would have us execute people as they worship?"

"Yes, if their prayers defy king and country."

Charlie said, "And when do we shoot them—before or after 'Amen'?"

Callum assumed an amiable tone. "Tavish, I'm sure you can't mean—"

Tavish cut him off sharply. "The penalty for refusing to take the oath of abjuration is summary execution."

Alex said, "Having the authority doesnae mean we're compelled to."

"Under my watch it does. Any man who refuses to renounce the covenant and acknowledge the king as his monarch and head of the church will be executed." Tavish scrutinized each man in turn. "And any soldier who refuses to follow orders will be found guilty of treason." Tavish waited as if hoping for someone to put him to the test, but silence fell upon them like a shroud.

There were dozens of parties like theirs, roaming the countryside, rooting out Covenanters. Tavish had received a tip that a minister was hiding out in a farm-house a short ride away. The ride felt much longer, given the unrelenting tension among the men. Callum had been in charge when they occupied Mari's farm. Their mission had been different. They had been sent to find Mari's brother, believed to be part of a group of assassins wanted for a murder near St. Andrews. Early on, they had determined that their man was not there, so they were to spy on the family and servants in hope of obtaining useful information. Callum did such a good job of gaining one person's confidence that she fell in love with him. However, even if a confrontation had occurred, execution would have been a last resort. His men felt the same way.

With Tavish in the lead, Callum and his men arrived at the farm. A young girl was out playing in the garden not far from the house. Tavish dismounted and walked over to her with a warm, gentle manner. "Hello, lassie. What is your name?"

She looked at him with wide, mistrusting eyes. "Elizabeth."

"Elizabeth." He gently nodded and stepped closer. "Look at your pretty, long hair."

Duncan caught Alex's eye. They had not been ordered to dismount, so they waited and watched.

Tavish stroked the girl's hair, and then wrapped it about his fist, pulling it tighter and tighter. "Is there a man staying here?"

She cried out, but did not answer. Her parents rushed out of the house. Tavish greeted them with a cool air of control. "Where is the minister? Bring him out." He kept twisting her hair. Silent tears fell down the girl's cheeks.

The father cried out, "Leave the child alone. She knows nothing."

"And you? What do you know?" asked Tavish.

"I know that you are wasting your time."

"Am I? Then prove it to me. Swear the oath."

His wife took in a sharp breath.

In a quiet voice, he said, "Good wife, we knew this day might come." He called out to the soldiers, "Let the child go. I know what you seek."

Tavish pulled out his pistol.

"God's blood!" said Callum. "Let the mother take the girl inside."

With a shove, Tavish released the child and loaded the pistol. He pointed the pistol at the farmer. "Where is the fugitive?"

The farmer's face drained of color.

From behind the croft, a man ran to the byre and threw himself on a horse.

"After him!" ordered Tavish, as he aimed his pistol at the farmer and fired. The shot hit its mark. The farmer's wife ran to her husband, while the daughter stood in the doorway.

Duncan, who was closest, gave chase as the minister rode away. Alex and Charlie followed, while Callum surveyed the scene grimly.

Tavish snarled, "What are you staring at?"

"My superior officer," answered Callum.

Taking his response as a show of respect, Tavish mounted his horse and rode off. Callum was close behind as they neared the woods. A riderless horse rode toward them from the trees.

Duncan had already dismounted and tethered his horse. Some birds flew up through the branches. Heads snapped in the direction they had come from.

Tavish fired, but missed. With a curse, he dismounted.

The minister emerged from behind a tree and ran. "Shoot him," said Tavish, as he arrived at Duncan's side.

Duncan drew his pistol from its holster beneath his left arm. He rammed the ball into the barrel, cocked it, and aimed it.

Tavish snapped at him as he loaded his own pistol. "What are you waiting for?" Tavish fired, but missed.

"He's getting away. Shoot him!" Tavish told Duncan.

Tavish cursed as he reloaded his rifle. Turning to Duncan, he yelled, "Fire when I tell you to fire."

Duncan cocked his pistol and fired, hitting branches high in the trees.

Tavish's pistol misfired. He growled. "The damn flint is too dull." Blood mottled his cheeks as he fired again. Sparks flew at him. With a curse, he clutched his face. "Go after him!"

The men all spent the next hour searching the woods.

"If you'd fired when I ordered you to, we'd have our man and be on our way home." Tavish scoffed as he searched through some shrubbery.

Duncan kept searching in stony silence.

The quieter Duncan was, the more Tavish fumed. "You're not nearly the soldier I thought you were."

Duncan fought to stay silent.

"Nor the man."

Duncan pulled his arm back to pound Tavish, when Alex caught Duncan's arm from behind in steely grip. "Would you look at this, Duncan?" He lowered his voice as he pulled him aside. "Steady." Alex steered Duncan away. "He's goading you."

"Aye, and a fine job he's doing. I would like to run him through with my dirk."

"But you willnae."

In the long silence that followed, Duncan seemed to consider it. "No, I willnae."

"Good. Because that castle back there has an oubliette that Tavish would love to throw you into. Think of Jenny."

Duncan seethed. "So am I just to smile and let him treat me like an errant hound?"

"Of course not. You dinnae have to smile." Alex grinned sympathetically.

"Be the better man that you are."

Duncan growled, "Sometimes you make too much sense."

Charlie joined them. "Perhaps we should look back toward the clearing. If your shot struck him, after all, he could be lying back there, and we missed him."

"He was not shot," said Duncan.

Alex scrutinized him. "You and I have hunted and fought in battles together. You're a very good shot."

Duncan smiled slyly. "Aye. I dinnae miss my target."

Charlie's eyes lit up with recognition for what Duncan was saying.

Duncan said, "Tavish can go hang himself, for I'll not shoot a man in cold blood just for praying."

A few yards away, Tavish cursed. "It's no use. We've lost him, thanks to Duncan's fine shooting."

Duncan opened his mouth to respond, but behind Tavish, leaves rustled. Tavish turned his head and stood still. He took a careful step, and then another. A few feet away, a white handkerchief rose from the bracken. Up came the minister with his hands in the air, frail and trembling. For the first time, they saw him up close. He was elderly, and taking in deep gulps of air.

Tavish pointed his pistol. "Say the oath."

The man closed his eyes as he said, "I cannae."

"Cannae or willnae?"

"Either," said the minister.

Tavish fired. The man's body jerked and went limp. The men stared in stunned silence. The man lay dead on the ground.

Tavish examined his gun. "This new flint worked much better." He put it away and turned to ride out of the woods.

"Are we not going to bury him?" asked Duncan.

Ignoring the question, Tavish rode out of the woods with an order for the others to follow. When they'd assembled out in the open, Tavish said, "The next time I tell you to fire, you will do it. Do you understand?"

Duncan looked at him squarely. "I understand you completely."

Tavish's eyes shifted from Duncan. "Dismount." When they all started to do so, Tavish said, "Only this one." His eyes narrowed as he looked toward Duncan, but he would not look him straight in the eye.

Duncan dismounted, as ordered.

Tavish said, "Bury him, if you like. And then think upon what I've said on your long walk home." With the butt of his rifle, he hit Duncan's horse on the rump, and the horse ran away. He then ordered the others leave with him. Duncan gave a firm nod to his friends to go on without him. They did, leaving Duncan alone.

For the rest of the day, the remaining men roamed the countryside watching for signs of Covenanter activity, but found none. At last, Tavish gave up for the day.

They found Duncan's horse wandering near the inn. With his horse in tow, they rode out to find Duncan before darkness fell.

They found Duncan running home with burning determination. If he had not been so tired, he would have looked triumphant. Instead, he mounted his horse and rode home as anger smoldered beneath his dark brow.

"Tavish is a most miserable wretch," Alex muttered.

Duncan shook his head. "No, I cannae agree."

Alex stared at him in disbelief.

"I'm as miserable, if not more so." Duncan tried but could not muster a smile.

Charlie said, "We can argue all evening about who was most miserable, but by my troth, the man is an ass. Can we all agree about that?"

"Aye," said Duncan, as the others laughed and agreed.

As they rode on toward the inn, the anger lifted, and an easy silence fell on them, until Charlie broke it. "Poor Jenny."

Duncan slowly turned toward him with a hooded gaze.

"All this while I've been feeling so sorry for her." His eyes flickered toward Duncan. "Yoked to you, as she is." Suppressing a grin, he continued. "But can you imagine her married to that whoreson?"

"I'd rather not," said Duncan, irritably.

Callum interrupted to change the subject. "Charlie, do you think it might rain?"

"We're in Scotland, man. What do you think?"

Callum rolled his eyes and gave Charlie a look. Alex laughed to himself.

Charlie saw them and, missing the point, shrugged it off.

When they arrived at the inn, Callum went upstairs to greet Jenny. They were late, and she did not know why.

"Where is Duncan?" she asked.

"He's downstairs in the pub."

"Downstairs. Is he not coming up here?"

"*Och*, of course he will."

Jenny eyed Callum. "Something is wrong. What has happened?"

"He's in one of his moods, that's all."

Jenny nodded and left. She found Duncan downstairs in the pub with a flagon of ale. He glanced at her, and returned to the drink in his hand.

"Duncan?" Jenny hooked her arm into his.

"I'm in no mood to talk."

Jenny stood at his side and watched him clench his jaw and stare down at his hands with a distant expression. She put her hand on his.

He reacted as though he had been hurt. "Did you not hear me?"

He glanced up toward the room, but Callum and Mari were there. He had no place to go. Grabbing her wrist, he led her outside. "I'll not leave you in there alone, but I meant what I said. Dinnae talk to me now."

She whispered, "I'm sorry." She watched him as though he were a stranger.

"Sorry? For what?"

"I'm sorry that you willnae talk to me."

His dark mood would not leave him. "Walk with me, if you must, but leave me alone. There's naught worth talking about."

Their walk brought them to a burn. They drank the cool water and rested beside it until Duncan's mood lifted.

Jenny slipped her hand into his. "Come, let us go sup with our friends."

DURING THAT SUPPER and the suppers to follow, Jenny watched Duncan withdraw more each day. While the others would talk over supper, Duncan was quiet, forcing a nod or a smile when he thought it was called for. As the days turned to weeks, his dark moods took over.

A second room opened up at the inn, leaving Jenny alone with Duncan and the brooding that was part of him now. Alex and Charlie found quarter with other troops, but would sup with their friends at day's end.

One night, on the way upstairs, Jenny said, "*Och!* I left my bonnet." She sent Duncan on and went back for her bonnet. With a glance up the stairs, she made sure that Duncan had gone to their room. She hurried outside and caught up with Alex and Charlie leading their horses from the stable.

Charlie's eyes gleamed. "So, you've finally decided to leave him. It was only a matter of time before my charms would overwhelm you."

Ordinarily, Jenny would have laughed at Charlie's remark, but this time, she could not.

This caught Alex's attention. "Jenny?"

She had no time to mince words. "What has happened to Duncan? Every day he grows worse."

Charlie said, "Has he not told you?"

"Told me what? You see how he is."

Alex said, "Ask him. It wouldnae be right for us to talk about things he has chosen to keep to himself."

Jenny clutched Alex's arm. "Do you think I've not asked? I may as well be a stranger for all he talks to me." She peered from one to the other. "Please, tell me the truth. Have I lost him?"

"Lost him? Dinnae be daft. Of course not, lass." Charlie exchanged glances with Alex.

Jenny fought to hold back her tears. "Then what is it? If there's somebody else, please tell me."

Alex lowered his chin and gazed earnestly at her. "Duncan loves you. Dinnae doubt that. Anything else should come from Duncan, himself."

Charlie said bluntly, "It's Tavish."

Alex eyed Charlie sharply, which raised Charlie's ire. "Do you honestly think Duncan will tell her? Look at her. Do you see how she suffers?"

Alex did look, and the sight softened his expression. "I'm sorry, hen, but I dinnae like to meddle."

"Then don't." Duncan stood a few feet away. "Come inside, Jenny." With a pointed glance toward Alex and Charlie, he took a firm hold of Jenny's upper arm and led her back into the inn.

Charlie raised an eyebrow and gave Alex a look as he shook his head. "She needed to know." With that, he mounted his horse and left.

Once inside their room, Duncan exploded. "Why must I go out in the night to find my wife? And then, when I find you, you're talking about things that should stay between us?"

"They're our friends. And I know of nothing between us anymore."

Her words struck him like a blunt blow, but he took it in silence. "Nothing? I've gone through hell for you, wife. And now you say there is nothing between us?"

"Nothing that you share with me. Whatever hell you have been through, you keep to yourself, and you leave me alone on the outside to wonder."

When his eyes were not shut, Duncan stared at the floor.

Jenny spoke softly. "I'm alone and unhappy, and I know that you're unhappy, too."

"Not with you. I couldnae be unhappy with you."

"But you are. Look at yourself. I do, every day. And I dinnae know what to do." Jenny reached out to touch him.

That one touch released his emotions. He pulled her into his arms and held her to him. "Jenny." He kissed her and stroked her hair. "I'm sorry."

Jenny circled her arms about his neck and held him close, as though he had returned from a faraway place. "Tell me about it."

"Why? What good would it do? You cannae fix this."

"I can listen. I can help carry the burden."

"If I cannae bear the weight, how can you?"

"My heart is strong." He turned and saw it shine through her eyes.

Duncan lifted her hands to his lips. "*Och*, Jenny. 'Tis hard to talk of such things."

"What things?"

Duncan pushed his hair back from his forehead and struggled to get the words out. "My weakness."

"Your what?"

He nodded. "Like my father. He would come home in his cups, and he'd cry to my mother and beg her to forgive him—like a whimpering pup. It made me sick to my stomach to see him like that."

Jenny searched his eyes. "But you're not like that."

"Nor will I be. If I cannae be man enough to take what life doles out to me, I am not much of a man."

"You are more of a man if you share it with your wife."

Duncan shook his head. "No, Jenny."

She took his face in her hands and held his gaze fiercely. "Yes, Jenny."

She had never spoken to him like that before. He was taken aback, but his face soon relaxed. He seemed almost to smile as she went on. "You will talk to me, Duncan. I'll not be locked out. If you'll not share all of your life, troubles included, I will leave you. Aye. For I'll not have part of a man."

Her strong warrior crumbled into her arms and buried his face in her chest. Jenny combed her fingers into his hair and kissed his head. Duncan looked up and kissed her with a fierceness that came from his soul. "I have wronged you."

Her eyes shimmered. "No, my braw man. You have wronged yourself."

They made love with a depth they had not known before. There had always been passion and love, but they found a place closer together, beyond the thrill that their bodies could share, to the joining of souls. In that place, there was power together that no human could conquer.

Afterward, they talked late into the night. Duncan told her what he had suffered and kept to himself in the weeks of unending harassment by Tavish.

"Do the others not speak up for you?"

"I forbade them. It would make me look weak. Besides which, they know that the man is a fool."

Jenny shook her head, closing her eyes. "I dinnae understand men."

"You understand me."

"I am not very certain of that." Jenny laughed.

"But you do. And yet, for some reason, you love me."

"I do that."

THEY AWOKE to a pounding on their door. Callum called out, "Duncan, are you coming?"

Duncan sat up and cursed. He gave Jenny a kiss as he pulled on his trews, and then called out to Callum, "Go on. I'll be along shortly."

Duncan arrived at the castle no more than a minute after Callum arrived.

"You're late," said Tavish.

"Not by much," Alex offered.

"I will tell that to the king when he asks why we've lost our next battle. I dare say he willnae find 'not by much' to be a satisfactory answer."

Duncan looked away, clenching his jaw, lest he say something he would surely regret. Instead, he kept his mind on Jenny and how much he loved her. He could endure anything for her.

Tavish went on. "We Highlanders are already thought to be a wild and undisciplined lot. I refuse to contribute to that perception." He called to the stable boy. "Take the morning off, lad."

The child's face lit with wonder. "Sorry, sir?"

"You heard me. Go on." Tavish grinned and waved him off. "You," He said, turning to Duncan just long enough for his disdain to strike its target. "Spend the day in the stables. You can start with the mucking."

Callum opened his mouth to protest, but Duncan silenced him with a glance. Alex and Charlie stole wary glances and then Tavish with disbelief.

Tavish pulled up straight in the saddle. "I do not suffer tardiness." He turned and rode off, and the others offered Duncan commiserative looks and then followed.

As they rode off, Duncan walked to the stables and set to work. He surveyed the task before him and let out a deep breath. The corner of his mouth turned up. What Tavish seemed to have forgotten was that Duncan had done these same tasks nearly all of his life. He knew how to work hard, and a day without Tavish was not such a bad thing. So he led the horses outside and tethered them there, and then picked up a pitchfork and shovel. As he worked, thoughts of Jenny and the absence of Tavish's voice served to brighten his day.

By the time Tavish returned, the stable was swept clean, with bed of fresh hay for each horse. It looked better than Duncan had ever seen it. Tavish scrutinized it, but could find no fault. So, with a sneer, he sent Duncan home.

Callum, Alex, and Charlie each promised him drinks when they got to the inn. Mari and Jenny joined them.

Jenny hugged him, but quickly leaned away. "Duncan! You smell terrible!"

"Do I? *Och*, Darlin', come here. Gie us a hug!" He

then locked her in an embrace as he buried his face in her neck. Jenny laughed as she begged him for mercy.

After Duncan washed up at Jenny's insistence, they all shared a meal, a few drams, and more laughter than they had in a long while.

THE NEXT MORNING, the four Clan MacDonell men were saddled and mounted when Tavish arrived. With barely a word, he led them out to the countryside for another day of searching for signs of rebellion that they had not seen since the minister escaped.

Charlie checked to make sure Tavish would not overhear them. "Do you ever wonder why we're here?"

"I know why we're here," answered Callum.

Alex said, "Aye, to quell the rebellion, but–"

"What rebellion?" asked Charlie.

With a nod, Alex said, "There it is. There is no rebellion."

"But we will be here if there ever is one," said Callum, with a crooked smile.

"But there is nothing to do!" Charlie said. "All we do is go on merry wee trots through flowery meadows."

Alex's eyes flickered toward Tavish before he leaned forward so as not to be overheard. "Oh, you can be sure that by the time Tavish reports it, we will have put down uprisings all across Galloway, and rooted out every dissenter who dared venture into Tavish's glorious presence."

"Aye, there's one now." Charlie nodded toward a

cow that was taking its time to amble in front of their path. They all chuckled as they crested the hill. In the valley below, some two dozen people had gathered. The men turned around to get back out of sight.

Tavish's eyes glimmered. "We will teach them not to flaunt acts of rebellion on my watch."

Callum said quietly, "I would hardly call it flaunting."

Tavish glared. "So says the man who married one of the rebels."

Callum said, "We'll not discuss my wife. As for the families down there in the valley, they are praying. They have done no one harm."

Tavish glowered at him. "Whose side are you on?"

Callum stared right back. "I fight for my clan and my king. Let no man dare doubt me." He said it almost like a threat.

Alex leaned closer. "Steady."

Callum added, "Lieutenant," as a show of respect.

With deliberate calm, Alex said, "There are women and children down there, and the men who are armed are but simple farmers. They pose no threat to us."

"All the better for us," said Tavish.

Callum said, "Why not send them back to their homes with a warning to not meet here again?"

Tavish held up his pistol. "Mr. Murdoch will warn them."

Alex said, "You cannae fire into the midst of innocent people."

"But I can, and you will. If they're here, they are not innocent."

Charlie said, "It's not right to ambush them like this."

Tavish said, "We have done so in battle."

Duncan shook his head. "These are not soldiers."

"No, they are rebels."

"With children," said Charlie.

"Whose parents chose to involve them in illegal activity." Tavish lifted his pistol. "Make ready, men."

Duncan reached for the pistol, but Tavish fired it first. Duncan grabbed it and flung it behind them.

Tavish turned to backhand him, but Duncan caught his wrist in a vice like grip. They both fell, fighting, from their horses. "I'll not murder for you." Duncan punched him. "I'll fight for the king, but I'll not murder children." Duncan struck him again.

"This is treason." Tavish fixed his eyes on Duncan. "One more word, and I'll have you court-martialed."

"You're not in a position to do that, at the moment." Duncan landed another blow, this time to Tavish's jaw.

The sound of horses drew Tavish's attention. "They're getting away. After them!"

"Go on," Alex told Callum and Charlie, as he tilted his head toward the rebels. "I'll see to this battle first. We'll catch up to you at the inn."

Duncan had Tavish pinned. He was no match for Duncan's skill and strength. Tavish struggled in vain. Alex watched Callum and Charlie ride away, but the fleeing Covenanters were already out of sight. He then turned his attention back to the row. Tavish had all this and more coming to him. Alex would not interfere with a fair fight.

Tavish freed a hand long enough to pull out his sgian dubh and thrust it at Duncan. Tavish pushed Duncan off, and stood up, with the bloody sgian dubh in his hand.

Alex cried, "God's wounds, Tavish! What have you done?"

"He refused to follow an order, and then he attacked his commanding officer."

"You didnae need to do that." Alex tore strips of his plaid to wrap around Duncan's wound.

"'Tis not so bad." Duncan winced.

Alex said, "You're lucky. He's just nicked your side." Flesh wound or not, he was losing blood.

"Good," said Tavish. "He'll be able to stand when I court-martial him." Tavish turned to check his horse's girth.

Duncan grabbed his shoulder and spun him around. He pounded him twice, and then Tavish fell to the ground. He lay unconscious.

"Do you know what you've done?" Alex helped Duncan to his horse.

"Aye. He deserved it."

"Yes, but you've made it worse for yourself."

"How so? He was already planning to court-martial me. What more could he do–kill me twice?"

Alex checked Tavish. He was breathing. "I'll send someone back for him." He and Duncan set out for the inn. "I'll tell him his horse ran off, so I had to go back for a cart to carry him."

"After you chased after me."

"Aye, that's better," said Alex.

Duncan said, "With luck, I'll have pounded the memory from his wee brain."

"Tavish? I doubt it."

With a dark laugh, Duncan said, "You could tell him that while he was chasing some nefarious Covenanter child, his horse threw him."

"Kicked him is more likely." Alex grinned.

Duncan shrugged. "No one could blame the horse."

Duncan's smile faded. "I will need to leave."

"Where will you go?"

"I can sign on with a merchant ship."

Alex gave a grim nod. "That might be best."

Duncan went on thinking aloud. "I will have to leave Jenny behind."

Chapter 15

Two Broken Coins

ON THEIR WAY TO THE INN, THEY FOUND JENNY AND Mari talking in hushed tones. Alex dismounted and left his horse with a stable boy, while Duncan veered off to a wooded area and tethered his horse to a tree near a burn.

Callum offered an arm to each lady and talked through his smile.

"Where is Duncan?"

"He'll join us upstairs."

"Why? What has happened?"

"Look calm, hen." Alex flashed a false smile. "We've been out for a pleasant stroll as far as anyone knows."

Jenny smiled back, but her eyes showed her alarm.

Alex said, "We cannae be seen with Duncan. Nor should you be heard speaking his name."

Once upstairs, Jenny rushed into the room and turned to Alex. Charlie, Callum and Mari followed him in and bolted the door.

"There was a disagreement," said Alex.

"A fight," Charlie corrected. "With Tavish."

Jenny gripped his arm. "Is he hurt?"

"It's a flesh wound."

A knock sounded at the door. "Jenny."

She rushed to the door, but Charlie got there first and opened it.

Jenny led a pale looking Duncan to the bed.

Callum said, "Tavish ordered him to fire into a gathering of innocent people. He was the first to refuse."

Jenny smoothed her hands over Duncan's face and then looked at the wound. She hurried to the basin of water, dipped a rag in it, and proceeded to look after Duncan.

He looked up at her as he took ragged breaths. "I must go."

Jenny nodded, not understanding.

"Alone, darlin'." He winced as she cleaned his wound. "I just came to say goodbye."

"No." Jenny stopped. "You'll not leave me."

"Mind me, Jenny. You must stay here with Callum and Mari."

"I willnae!" Eyes blazing, she finished wrapping a bandage about him.

With a glance outside, Charlie nodded to the others. It was nearly dark. When the barkeep was busy, Duncan walked downstairs surrounded by the three men, who propped him up when he faltered. Jenny followed, barely hiding her distress.

As they walked past the stable on the way to Duncan's horse, Jenny hooked her arm about Charlie's and held him back while the others walked on. "I love you like a brother, but God help me, I'll fight you like one if you dinnae lend me your horse."

Charlie's eyes opened wide.

"WHAT THE DEVIL!" said Duncan, as Charlie walked his horse through the woods, with Jenny upon it.

With a glint in his eye, Charlie said, "I'll not fight her. She's tougher than you."

"You've no time to linger," said Alex.

Duncan's gaze burned through Jenny.

She lifted her chin. "I'll not mind you. I will go where you go, and I'll not change my mind."

His dark eyes warmed as he looked upon her. "Darlin', I know that I used to tell you to speak up for yourself more, but–"

Her eyes shone. "Aye, and I'm minding you now."

Despite his stern look, he said nothing.

Jenny's lips spread to a warm smile.

Callum handed Duncan a pouch of coins, and the others added theirs to it. "With luck, you can board ship and hide out for the night. Knowing Tavish, the harbor will be crawling with dragoons by the morning."

Charlie cursed. "He's coming. He's got two dragoons in tow."

They escaped down a wynd just as Tavish rode up to the inn.

"Search it," he ordered the two dragoons riding with him. While they went into the inn, Charlie and

Alex joined him. With an easy smile, Alex said, "So they found you. You're looking much better."

"Aye, and I'll soon be even better." Tavish turned toward the inn. As he did, Callum and Mari circled behind the stable and approached from behind, strolling hand-in-hand.

Mari said, "Lieutenant MacLean, won't you come inside for a visit. We so rarely have the pleasure."

"I'm afraid not, Mistress MacDonell." He took in a breath to say something, but instead studied them. With increasing suspicion, he said, "Where is he?"

Charlie looked genuinely puzzled, while Alex tipped his head and peered back.

Callum spoke slowly to stall him. "Well, Tavish—"

"Lieutenant MacLean," Tavish corrected.

With a nod, Callum grinned and said, "Of course. We've known each other so long that I forget sometimes. You are a superior officer, and due the respect accorded by your rank. I sincerely apologize for the oversight—"

"Dammit, where is he?"

Callum said, "Duncan? I dinnae know. We rode after him, but we never found him."

Alex said, "We thought it best to send some men to bring you back safely, and resume the search later."

"I don't care what you thought. You've allowed him to escape."

"He was not here when we got here."

Alex said, "If he turns up, I am sure he'll want to apologize. I'm certain that you will put it behind you. You're a fair man."

Something stuck in Charlie's throat, making him cough.

Tavish glowered. "The man has affronted me too many times. He defied an order, warned the enemy, and attacked his superior officer."

Callum nodded in seeming agreement. "We can talk in the morning. When you've had some rest, things will fall into perspective."

Tavish eyed Callum. "What sort of perspective does it take to recognize treason? We will find him, and we will court-martial him."

DAWN BROKE and Tavish's men stood guard over the docks of Portpatrick. They had spent the night scouring the docks, every ship, and the taverns and inns. They now stood guard at each ship and watched every sailor, dock worker, and pushcart vendor as the sun rose to warm the crisp autumn morning.

Charlie kept an eye on the soldiers with Alex. "If they went over land, then they travel on foot, for they left the horses where Duncan said they would."

"They must be hiding somewhere," said Alex.

Charlie watched a pair of dragoons come out of a shop they had searched. "I hope they hid well. Tavish willnae give up."

"Poor Jenny." Alex stared absently out at the increasing activity. "She doesnae know what she's gotten herself into."

"I think she does well enough." Charlie stared out over the water. "Love is a powerful thing."

Alex turned eyed Charlie as though he were a stranger. "What is this? Are you waxing romantic?"

Charlie sneered. "Nay, dinnae be daft."

The dock was alive with activity now. Pushcarts were loaded and cargo was stacked up, unloaded or waiting to be shipped out. A first mate barked orders as his crew straggled into queue at the gangplank that led up to a ship.

Charlie chuckled. "I hope that sorry lot had a good time last night."

Alex shook his head. "From the looks of them, they're paying for it this morning." He looked away until something caught his eye. "Charlie, what do you see?"

"The same thing we've been looking at all morning."

"Look closer," said Alex.

One-by-one Charlie described the newly arrived sailors queuing up at their ship. "Old sailor, stocky sailor, sailor I wouldnae want to make angry, tall sailor, cabin boy—what the devil?"

Alex shushed him.

"Brilliant," said Charlie.

The tall sailor wore English clothing. He cast a sideways look at Alex and Charlie as he tugged his cap down on his face. Beside him, a boy with a dirt-smudged face shoved his hands into his pockets and faced the ship with his eyes to the ground. Alex and Charlie sank further into the shadows. Tavish sent more dragoons over to inspect the sailors. Alex's eyes narrowed.

Without a word, Charlie ducked into the tavern

beside them. Sailors started boarding the ship. The queue of sailors moved forward. As Duncan and Jenny drew close to the dragoons, Charlie returned.

"This is a fine time to relieve yourself, Charlie."

"It was a fine time. Whether it is a relief remains to be seen." Charlie kept his hand near his pistol and watched.

A pretty barmaid emerged from the tavern, her creamy breasts bouncing with each step she took toward the sailors.

"What is she doing?" Alex asked.

"Saying farewell to her sweetheart?" Charlie tilted his head and watched with a gleam in his eye.

She looked as though she were heading for Duncan, but stopped a few sailors behind him. A young dragoon took a step forward to stop her, but hesitated, transfixed by the sight of her well-rounded beauty up close. She threw her arms about a stunned sailor as her unfettered linen-clad flesh fluffed from her bodice and pressed against him. His hands flexed in the air for a moment, but surrendered and circled her waist. A handkerchief fluttered to the ground. She bent over, plump bottom up, to retrieve it. As she stood, she looked down and said, "Oh!" With a coy pout, she pressed her swelling mounds back into her bodice. She dabbed her eye with the handkerchief and then pressed it into his hand. "Remember me, love."

His look of wonder as she walked away left no doubt that he would do just that.

By this time, Duncan and Jenny were on board, out of sight. The barmaid walked past Charlie and winked. In return, he gave her an approving grin. "Please excuse me," said Charlie.

"Nature calling again?" Alex smirked.

Charlie laughed. "Aye, nature." Charlie clapped his hand on Alex's shoulder. "Dinnae wait for me." He disappeared inside the tavern.

THE SHIP PULLED out of the harbor with a sailor and cabin boy at the ship's rail. As they watched Port-patrick grow smaller, Duncan's hand barely touched Jenny's as they held onto the rail.

He could not resist a smile as he stole a sideways glance at his Jenny dressed as a boy. She would have to remain so until they left the ship.

Duncan forced his gaze straight ahead. "I hear that, on a clear day, you can see Scotland from the coast of Ireland in places."

"Can you really?"

"So I've heard."

Jenny played with the coin that hung from her neck and smiled to imagine it.

Duncan stole one more look. "We'll settle there by the water. At day's end, we'll look out at the sea. I'll hold you in my arms, and like two broken coins, we'll be whole."

Jenny lifted her face to the wind.

The Highland Soldiers Series

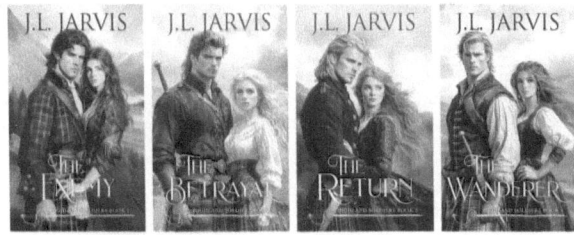

Highland Soldiers: Scottish historical romances set during turbulence seventeenth-century Scotland

Thank You!

Thank you for reading! If you enjoyed this book, please consider leaving a review or a rating. Your feedback on bookstore, Goodreads, and Bookbub websites helps other readers discover books they'll enjoy.

instagram.com/jljarvis.writer

facebook.com/jljarvis1writer

x.com/JLJarvis_writer

youtube.com/@jljarvis-author

goodreads.com/jljarvis

bookbub.com/authors/j-l-jarvis

Also by J.L. Jarvis

Waterfront Summers

(Can be read in any order)

The Cottage at Peregrine Cove

The House on Serenity Lake

Moonlight on Mariner's Bluff

Drake & Wilde Mysteries

(Reading Order)

Love in the Time of Pumpkins

Secrets in the Hollow

Shadow of the Horseman

Standalones

(Can be read in any order)

A Cowboy Kind of Love

A Christmas Eve Stop

Christmas by Lamplight

A Kiss in the Rain

App-ily Ever After

Once Upon a Winter

The Red Rose

Highland Vow

Short Stories

(Can be read in any order)

The Magic of Snow

The Eleventh-Hour Pact

A Christmas Yarn

The Farmer and the Belle

Work-Crush Balance

Cedar Creek

(Can be read in any order)

Christmas at Cedar Creek

Snowstorm at Cedar Creek

Sunlight on Cedar Creek

Pine Harbor

(Reading Order)

Allison's Pine Harbor Summer

Evelyn's Pine Harbor Autumn

Lydia's Pine Harbor Christmas

Holiday House

(Can be read in any order)

The Christmas Cabin

The Winter Lodge

The Lighthouse

The Christmas Castle

The Beach House

The Christmas Tree Inn

The Holiday Hideaway

Highland Passage

(Can be read in any order)

Highland Passage

Knight Errant

Lost Bride

Highland Soldiers

(Reading Order)

The Enemy

The Betrayal

The Return

The Wanderer

American Hearts

(Can be read in any order)

Secret Hearts

Forbidden Hearts

Runaway Hearts

For more information, visit jljarvis.com.

Get monthly book news at news.jljarvis.com.

About the Author

J.L. Jarvis is a left-handed former opera singer/teacher/lawyer who writes books. She now lives and writes on a mountaintop in upstate New York.

jljarvis.com